HARLEQUIN
Presents

Welcome to a month of fantastic reading, brought to you by Harlequin Presents! Continuing our magnificent series THE ROYAL HOUSE OF NIROLI is Melanie Milburne with *Surgeon Prince, Ordinary Wife*. With the first heir excluded from the throne of Niroli, missing prince and brilliant surgeon Dr. Alex Hunter is torn between duty and his passion for a woman who can never be his queen.... Don't miss out!

Also for your reading pleasure is the first book of Sandra Marton's new THE BILLIONAIRES' BRIDES trilogy, *The Italian Prince's Pregnant Bride*, where Prince Nicolo Barbieri acquires Aimee Black, who, it seems, is pregnant with Nicolo's baby! Then favorite author Lynne Graham brings you a gorgeous Greek in *The Petrakos Bride*, where Maddie comes face-to-face again with her tycoon idol....

In *His Private Mistress* by Chantelle Shaw, Italian racing driver Rafael is determined to make Eden his mistress once more...while in *One-Night Baby* by Susan Stephens, another Italian knows nothing of the secret Kate is hiding from their one night together. If a sheikh is what gets your heart thumping, Annie West brings you *For the Sheikh's Pleasure*, where Sheikh Arik is determined to get Rosalie to open up to receive the loving that only *he* can give her! In *The Brazilian's Blackmail Bargain* by Abby Green, Caleb makes Maggie an offer she just can't refuse. And finally Lindsay Armstrong's *The Rich Man's Virgin* tells the story of a fiercely independent woman who finds she's pregnant by a powerful millionaire. Look out for more brilliant books next month!

BILLIONAIRES' BRIDES
Pregnant by their princes…

Take three incredibly wealthy European princes and match them with three beautiful, spirited women. Add large helpings of intense emotion and passionate attraction. Result: three unexpected pregnancies…and three possible princesses—if those princes have their way…

THE ITALIAN PRINCE'S PREGNANT BRIDE
Available in August

THE GREEK PRINCE'S CHOSEN WIFE
Available in September

THE SPANISH PRINCE'S VIRGIN BRIDE
Available in October

Sandra Marton

THE ITALIAN PRINCE'S PREGNANT BRIDE

BILLIONAIRES' BRIDES
Pregnant by their princes…

HARLEQUIN®

TORONTO • NEW YORK • LONDON
AMSTERDAM • PARIS • SYDNEY • HAMBURG
STOCKHOLM • ATHENS • TOKYO • MILAN • MADRID
PRAGUE • WARSAW • BUDAPEST • AUCKLAND

ISBN-13: 978-0-373-12652-1
ISBN-10: 0-373-12652-2

THE ITALIAN PRINCE'S PREGNANT BRIDE

First North American Publication 2007.

www.eHarlequin.com

Printed in U.S.A.

All about the author...
Sandra Marton

SANDRA MARTON wrote her first novel while she
was still in elementary school. Her doting parents
told her she'd be a writer someday and Sandra
believed them. In high school and college, she wrote
dark poetry nobody but her boyfriend understood,
though looking back, she suspects he was just being
kind. As a wife and mother, she wrote murky short
stories in what little spare time she could manage,
but not even her boyfriend-turned-husband could
pretend to understand those. Sandra tried her hand
at other things, among them teaching and serving
on the board of education in her hometown, but the
dream of becoming a writer was always in her heart.

At last Sandra realized she wanted to write books
about what all women hope to find: love with
that one special man, love that's rich with fire and
passion, love that lasts forever. She wrote a novel,
her very first, and sold it to the Harlequin Presents
line. Since then, she's written more than sixty books,
all of them featuring sexy, gorgeous, larger-than-life
heroes. A four-time RITA® Award finalist, she has also
received five *Romantic Times BOOKreviews* awards
for Best Harlequin Presents of the Year and has been
honored with a *Romantic Times BOOKreviews*
Career Achievement Award for Series Romance.

Sandra lives with her very own sexy, gorgeous,
larger-than-life hero in a sun-filled house on a quiet
country lane in the northeastern United States.

CHAPTER ONE

SHE came hurrying along the sidewalk, enveloped from head to toe in black suede, stiletto-heeled boots clicking sharply, her head bent against the rain-driven wind, and barreled into Nicolo just as he stepped from the taxi.

The doorman moved forward but Nicolo had already dropped his briefcase and caught her by the shoulders.

"Easy," he said pleasantly.

Her hood fell back as she looked up at him. Nicolo, always appreciative of beauty, smiled.

She was beautiful, with elegant bones, a mouth that looked soft and inviting, and eyes the deep blue of spring violets, all that framed by a mass of honey-colored loose curls.

If someone had to run you down, this was surely the woman an intelligent man would choose.

"Are you all right?"

She pulled out of his grasp. "I'm fine."

"My fault entirely," he said graciously. "I should have watched where I was—"

"Yes," the woman said, "you should have."

He blinked. She was looking at him with total disdain. His smile faded. Though he was Roman, he'd spent a good part of his life in Manhattan. He understood that civility was not an art here but it was *she* who'd run into *him*.

"I beg your pardon, *signorina,* but—"

"But then," she said coldly, "I suppose people like you think you own the street."

Nicolo lifted his hands from her shoulders with exaggerated care.

"Look, I don't know what your problem is, but—"

"You," she said crisply, "are my problem."

What was this? A Mona Lisa with the temperament of a hellcat. Innate old-world gallantry warred with new-world attitude.

Attitude won.

"You know," he said brusquely, "I apologized to you when there was no need, and you speak to me as if I were scum. You could use some manners."

"Just because I'm a woman—"

"Is that what you are?" His smile was as cold as his words. "Let's see about that, shall we?" Temper soaring, logic shot to hell, Nicolo pulled the blonde to her toes and kissed her.

It lasted less than a second. Just a quick brush of his mouth over hers. Then he let go of her, had the satisfaction of seeing those violet eyes widen in astonishment…

And caught the rich, sweet taste of her on his lips.

Sweet heaven. Had he gone *un po'pazzo?*

He had to be. Only a crazy man would haul a mean-tempered woman into his arms on Fifth Avenue.

"You," she said, "you—you—"

Oh, but it had been worth it. Look at her now, sputtering like a steam engine, that icy demeanor completely shattered.

She jerked free of his hands. Her arm rose. She was going to slap him; he could read it in those amazing eyes, eyes that flashed lethal bolts of lightning. He probably deserved it—but he'd be damned if he'd let her do it.

He bent his head toward hers. "Hit me," he said softly, "and I promise, I'll make your world come crashing down around your ears."

Her lips formed a phrase he would not have imagined women knew. Not the women in his world, at any rate, but then none of them would have accused a man of something clearly their fault.

Why be modest? The truth was, not a woman he'd ever met would have blamed him even if he were at fault.

The hellcat glared at him. He returned the look. Then she swept past him, honey-blond mane glittering with raindrops, black suede coat billowing after her like a sail.

He watched her go until she was lost in the umbrella-shrouded crowd hurrying through the chilly March rain.

Then he took a deep breath and turned his back to her.

His eyes met the doorman's. Nothing. Not the slightest acknowledgment that anything the least bit unusual had happened but then, this was New York. New Yorkers had long ago learned it was wisest not to know anything.

And a damned good thing for him.

Kissing her had been bad enough. Challenging her to call the police...

Nicolo shuddered.

How stupid could a man be? He could have ended up with his face spread across Page Six. Not exactly the publicity one wanted before a meeting with the ninety-year-old head of an investment firm that prided itself on decorum and confidentiality.

The rain was coming down harder.

The doorman already had his suitcase. Nicolo picked up his briefcase and walked into the hotel.

His suite was on the forty-third floor, which gave him an excellent view of the park and the skyline beyond it.

When he started looking for a permanent place to live in the city, he'd want a view like this.

Nicolo tossed his raincoat on a chair. If all went well, he'd contact a Realtor after Monday's meeting.

If? There was no "if" about it. The word wasn't in his lexicon. He never went after something without making damned sure he knew when, where and how to get it. That approach was a key to his success.

He toed off his shoes, stripped away his clothes and headed for the shower.

He was fully prepared for Monday's meeting and his long-anticipated buyout of Stafford-Coleridge-Black.

His financial empire was huge, with offices in London, Paris, Singapore, and, of course, Rome.

It was time for Barbieri International to move into the New York market. For that, he wanted something that would be the crown jewel of his corporation.

In the rarefied echelon of private banking, that could only be Stafford-Coleridge-Black, whose client list read like a Who's Who of American wealth and power.

Only one thing stood in the way: SCB's chairman, James Black.

"I have no idea what you'd think to discuss with me," the old man had said when he'd finally agreed to take Nicolo's phone call.

"I've heard rumors," Nicolo had answered carefully, "that you are considering a change."

"You mean," Black had said bluntly, "you've heard that I'm going to die soon. Well, I assure you, sir, I am not."

"What I have heard," Nicolo had said, "is that a man of your good judgment believes in planning ahead."

Black had made a sound that might have been a laugh.

"Touché, Signore Barbieri. But I assure you, any changes I might make would be of no interest to you. We are family owned and have been for more than two hundred years. The bank has been passed from one generation to another." A brief, barely perceptible pause. "But I wouldn't expect you to understand the importance of that."

Nicolo had thought how good it was that they were not face-to-face. Even so, he had to work hard to control his temper. Black was an old man but he was in full command of his faculties. What he'd said had to be a deliberate, if thinly veiled, insult.

This high up the ladder, the international financial community was like an exclusive club. People knew things about each other and what Black knew was that Nicolo's wealth and stature, despite his title, had not come from legacy and inheritance but had been solely self-created.

As far as the James Blacks of this world were concerned, that was not a desirable image.

Probably not desirable as far as Fifth Avenue honeyblondes were concerned, either, Nicolo mused, and wondered where in hell that thought had come from?

What mattered, all that mattered this weekend, was his business with Black. It had mattered enough during that phone call to keep his tone neutral when he responded to the flinty old bastard's gibe.

"On the contrary," Nicolo had said. "I *do* understand. Completely. I believe in maintaining tradition." He'd paused, weighing each word. "I also believe you would do your institution a disservice if you refuse to hear what I have to say."

He'd gambled that Black would bite. Not that it was all that much of a gamble, considering what Nicolo knew.

SCB had, indeed, always been family-owned and operated. The problem was that the old man was facing his ninetieth birthday and his sole heir was a grandchild still in school.

Still in school…and a girl.

Nicolo was sure that "tradition," to James Black, meant handing the reins of the company to an heir, not an heiress. Black had never made a secret of his feelings about women in business.

And that was probably the one thing the two men could agree on, Nicolo mused as he stepped from the shower. It was what he would build his argument on, Monday morning.

Women were too emotional. They were unpredictable and undisciplined. They did well as assistants, even, on occasion, as heads of departments, but as ultimate decision-makers?

Not until science figured out a way women could overcome the dizzying up-and-down ride of their hormones.

It wasn't their fault—it was simply a fact of life.

And that, Nicolo thought as he dressed in gray flannel trousers, a black cashmere turtleneck and mocs, was his ace in the hole.

Nicolo was the only investor who could afford the indulgence of buying SCB privately. That meant that Black had nowhere to turn except to him, unless he wanted to sell his venerable institution to one of the giant conglomerates hungering for it, then live long enough to see it disappear within the corporate maw.

He was the old man's salvation and they both knew it. The moment of truth had come last week when Black's secretary phoned and said her employer would agree to a brief meeting solely as a courtesy.

"Of course," Nicolo had said calmly but when he hung up, he'd pumped his fist in victory.

The meeting meant only one thing: the old man had admitted defeat and would sell to him. Oh, he'd undoubtedly make him dance through a couple of hoops first, but how bad could that be?

Nicolo slipped on a leather bomber jacket and shut the door to his suite behind him.

He wouldn't dance, but he'd move his feet in time to the music. Do just enough to placate the old bastard.

Then Stafford-Coleridge-Black would be his.

Not bad for a boy who'd grown up in not-so-genteel poverty, Nicolo thought, and pressed the button for the elevator.

The rain had stopped, though the skies were gray and soggy.

The doorman flagged a cab.

"Sixty-third off Lexington," Nicolo told the driver.

He was meeting friends at the Eastside Club. The three of them had agreed, via e-mail yesterday, on the benefits of a quick workout, especially since both Nicolo and Damian had just flown in.

Private planes or not, a man felt his muscles tighten after a seemingly interminable international flight.

Then they'd go somewhere quiet for dinner and catch up on old times. He was looking forward to that. He, Damian and Lucas had known each other forever. For thirteen years, ever since they'd met at a pub just off the Yale campus, three eighteen-year-old kids from three different parts of the world, all of them wondering how in hell they'd survive in this strange country.

Survive? They'd flourished. And formed a tight friendship. They saw each other less frequently now, thanks to their individual business interests, but they were still best pals.

And still single, which was exactly how they all wanted it. In fact, they always began the evening with the same toast.

"Life," Lucas would say solemnly, "is short."

"And marriage," Damian would add even more solemnly, "is forever."

The last part of the toast was left to Nicolo.

"And freedom," he'd say dramatically, "freedom, gentlemen, is everything!"

He was smiling as his cab pulled up in front of the Eastside Club. It was housed in what had once been a block of nineteenth-century brownstones that had been gutted, completely made over and combined into one structure.

A very exclusive health club.

The Eastside didn't advertise. No plaque or sign identified it to passersby. Membership was by invitation only, reserved for those who valued privacy and could afford the steep fees that guaranteed it.

For all that, the club was completely lacking in pretension. There were no trendy exercise gadgets, no bouncy music, and the only part of the gym with a mirrored wall was the free-weight area so that you could check your reflection to see if you were lifting properly.

What there were, in addition to the weights, were punching bags, a pool and a banked indoor track.

Best of all, the Eastside was for men only.

Women were a distraction. Besides, Nicolo thought as he inserted his key card in the front door lock, it was a relief to get away from them for a while.

He had enough women to deal with in his life. Too many, he sometimes thought, when ending a relationship led to tears. He was, he'd heard whispered, "an excellent catch." He scoffed at that but to himself, he admitted it was probably true.

Why not be honest?

"Good evening, Mr. Barbieri. Nice to see you again, sir."

"Jack," Nicolo said amiably. He signed in and headed for the locker room.

He had money. A private jet. Cars. He owned a ski lodge in Aspen, an oceanfront estate on Mustique, a *pied-a-terre* in Paris and, of course, there was the *palazzo* in Rome, the one that had supposedly come to the Barbieri family through Julius Caesar.

That was what his great-grandmother had always claimed.

Nicolo thought it more likely it had come to them through a thief in Caesar's time, but he'd never contradicted her. He'd loved the old woman as he'd never loved anyone else. He'd always been grateful he'd made his first million and restored the ancient but decrepit *Palazzo di Barbieri* before she'd died.

Her pleasure had brought joy to his heart.

He'd liked making her happy. In fact, he liked making most women happy.

It was only when their demands became unreasonable, when they began to talk of The Future, of The Importance of Settling Down—and he could almost actually feel the physical weight they put into the phrase when it tumbled from their lips—that Nicolo knew that Making Them Happy wasn't as important as Not Making a Commitment.

No way. Not him. Not yet.

For an evening? Of course. A week? Yes. Even a month. Two months. Hell, he wasn't the kind of man to jump from bed to bed….

What would the woman in the black suede coat be like in bed? A honey-maned tigress? Or an ice queen?

Not that he gave a damn. It was simply a matter of intellectual curiosity.

He liked women who enjoyed their femininity. Enjoyed being appreciated by a man.

Nicolo hung his things in his locker.

It didn't take a psychiatrist to figure out that the tigress was not such a woman. Although, in the bed of the right man, perhaps she could be.

The mane of hair. The delicate oval face. The amazing eyes, that tender mouth. And, yes, he'd felt its tenderness even in that brush of his lips against hers...

Fantastico.

Hell. He was giving himself a hard-on over a woman who'd insulted him, who he would never see again. He didn't want to think about her or any woman. Not this weekend. No distractions. No sex. Like an athlete, he believed in abstinence before going *mano a mano.*

He needed to focus on Monday's meeting.

Nicolo pulled on gray cotton running shorts, a sleeveless, ancient Yale sweatshirt and a pair of Nikes.

A hard, sweaty workout was just what he needed.

The gym was almost empty. Well, it was Saturday night. Only one other guy was in the vast room, pounding around the track with the lonely intensity of the dedicated runner.

Damian.

Nicolo grinned, trotted over and fell in alongside him.

"Any slower," he said, picking up the pace, "we'd be walking. You getting too old to run fast?"

Damian, who at thirty-one was exactly the same age as Nicolo, shot him a deadpan look.

"I'll call the paramedics when you collapse."

"Big talk."

"A hundred bucks says I can beat you."

"Twenty times around?"

"Forty," Nicolo said, and shot away.

Moments later, they finished in a dead heat and turned to each other, breathing hard and grinning from ear to ear.

"How's Rome?" Damian said.

"How's Athens?"

The men's grins widened and they clasped each other in a bear hug.

"Man," Damian said, "you're a sweaty bastard."

"You're not exactly an ad for *GQ*."

"How was your flight?"

Nicolo took a couple of towels from a stand beside the track and tossed one to Damian.

"Fine. Some weather just before we landed, but nothing much. Yours?"

"The same," Damian said, wiping his face. "I really like this little Learjet I bought."

"Little," Nicolo said, laughing.

"Well, it's still not as big as yours."

"Mine's always going to be bigger than yours, Aristedes."

"You wish."

It was an old line of banter and made them grin again.

"So," Nicolo said, "where's Lucas?"

"We're meeting him in—" Damian looked at his watch. "In two hours."

"You guys picked a restaurant?"

"Well, more or less."

Nicolo raised an eyebrow. "Meaning?"

"Meaning," Damian said, "our old friend bought himself a club. Downtown. *The* club of the minute, he says."

"Meaning, crowded. Noisy. Lots of music, lots of booze, lots of spectacular-looking women out for a good time…"

"Sounds terrible," Damian said solemnly.

Nicolo smiled as he draped his towel around his shoulders. "Yeah, I know. But I have an important meeting Monday morning."

"Well, so do I."

"Very important."

Damian looked at him. "So?"

"So," Nicolo said, after a moment, "I'm hoping to finalize a deal. With James Black."

"Whoa. That *is* important. So, tonight we celebrate in advance, at Lucas's place."

"Well, I want to stay focused. Get to bed at a decent hour tonight and tomorrow night. No liquor. No distractions—"

"*Thee Mou!* Don't tell me! No sex?"

Nicolo shrugged. "No sex."

"Sex is not a distraction. It's exercise. Good for the heart."

"It's bad for the concentration."

"That's BS."

"We believed it when we played soccer, remember? And we won."

"We won," Damian said dryly, "because the competition was lousy."

"I'm serious."

"So am I. Giving up sex is against the laws of nature."

"Idiot," Nicolo said fondly. The men walked to the free weights area and made their selections. "It's just a matter of discipline."

"Unless, of course, there was such an instant attraction you couldn't walk away." Damian grunted as he lifted a pair of twenty-pound weights. "And how often is that about to happen?"

"Never," Nicolo answered—and, unbidden, the image of the blonde with the hot eyes and the cold attitude flashed before his eyes.

He had been reaching for the twenty-pound weights, too. Instead he lifted a pair of heavier ones and worked with them until his mind was a pain-filled blank.

* * *

Farther downtown, in a part of Manhattan that was either about to be discovered or still a slum, depending on a buyer's point of view, Aimee Stafford Coleridge Black slammed her apartment door behind her, tossed her black suede coat at a chair and kicked off her matching boots.

The coat slid off the chair. The boots bounced off the wall. Aimee didn't give a damn.

Amazing, how a day that began so filled with promise could end so badly.

Aimee marched into the kitchen, filled the kettle with water, put it on to boil and changed her mind. The last thing she needed was a caffeine buzz.

She was buzzing enough without it, thanks to her grandfather.

Why had he summoned her to his office, if not to make the announcement she'd been anticipating?

"I shall retire next May," he'd told her almost a year ago, "when I reach ninety, at which time I shall place Stafford-Coleridge-Black in the charge of the person who will guide it through its next fifty years. A person who will, of course, carry on the Stafford-Coleridge-Black lineage."

Lineage. As important to James as breathing but that was fine because she, Aimee, was the only person with both the necessary lineage and the proper education to assume command.

She had a bachelor's degree in finance. A master's degree in business. She'd spent her summers since high school interning at SCB.

She knew more about the bank than anyone, maybe even including Grandfather, who still believed in a world devoid of computers and e-mail.

Aimee marched into the bedroom and methodically stripped off the gray wool suit and white silk blouse she'd deemed appropriate for the meeting with Grandfather this afternoon. She'd wanted to look businesslike, even though she knew damned well you could do as much business in jeans as you could in Armani.

She'd even worked up a little speech of assurance about how she wouldn't change a thing, though she'd mentally crossed her fingers because there were things that definitely needed changing.

She'd presented herself at his office precisely at four. James was a stickler for promptness. She'd kissed his papery cheek, sat down as directed, folded her hands…

And listened as he told her he had not yet reached a decision as to who would replace him.

Be calm, she'd told herself. And she had been, or at least she'd managed to seem calm as she asked him what decision there was to make.

"You already said it would be me, Grandfather."

"I said it would be someone capable," James said briskly. "Someone of my lineage."

"Well—"

The look on his face had frozen her with horror. "You don't mean…Bradley?"

Bradley. Her cousin. Or her something. Who understood the complexities of second cousins twice removed, or whatever the hell he was? Bradley had been wimping around the bank for years, interning the same as she had, except he'd never done a day's work, never done anything except try to grope her in the stockroom.

"Not Bradley," she'd finally breathed.

"Bradley has a degree in economics."

Yes. From a college that probably also gave degrees in basket-weaving.

"He's well-spoken."

He was, once he had three or four straight vodkas in him.

"And," her grandfather had said, saving the best for last, "he is a man."

A man. Meaning, nature's royalty. A prince, whereas she was a lesser creature because she was female.

Grandfather had risen to his feet, indicating that she was no longer welcome in the royal presence.

"Be here Monday morning, Aimee. Ten o'clock sharp. I'll announce my decision then."

Dismissed, just like that.

Sent out the door, down the wheezing old elevator, into the street where she'd walked blindly, no idea where in hell she was or where she was going, which was why she hadn't seen the man and he'd almost knocked her down.

That despicable, horrible man who'd insisted it was she who'd walked into him. Who'd accused her of not being a woman when, damn him, it was the very fact that she *was* a woman that was going to deny her the one thing she wanted in life.

What a fool she'd been. What an idiot. She'd turned down two wonderful job offers because she'd believed— she'd been stupid enough to believe—

She'd been anguishing over that when the man charged into her.

As if she were invisible, which she undoubtedly was because she was female. Oh, the arrogance of men. Of him. The way he'd clasped her shoulders and looked down at her from the lofty heights of his lofty maleness.

"Easy," he'd said, and smiled, and that—the smile, the slight foreign huskiness to the word, the broad shoulders, the ink-black hair, the midnight-blue eyes and the face that was the male equivalent of what had launched a thousand ships, *that* was supposed to make up for his rudeness?

Aimee had told him what she thought of him.

Men didn't like honesty. She'd learned that a long time ago. And this one, this—this bad-mannered stranger, had decided she needed a lesson, that she needed a graphic reminder of her place in the universe…

He'd kissed her.

Kissed her! Put his mouth on hers, the arrogant, miserable son of a bitch….

His firm mouth. His soft mouth. His mouth that was, any woman could tell, made for long, deep kisses…

God, she was in bad shape. Anger, adrenaline, whatever you called it, was pumping through her veins. She was completely stressed out.

A man would know what to do to ease such stress.

He'd go to a gym and sweat it out. Actually that would work for her, too, but her gym, a gym for women, was closed. Hey, it was Saturday. Date night for the fairer sex, right?

"Such crap," Aimee said.

She could almost feel the steam coming out of her ears.

Or a man would call up his buddies, meet them someplace crowded and noisy and guzzle beer. That's what men under pressure did, didn't they? Go out, drink, talk about stupid things, pick up women?

Sex was the great relaxer. Everybody said so. Okay, not her because she'd had sex and it had been far from memorable but according to everything she'd read, sex could lower your stress levels every time.

Aimee snorted.

Imagine if a woman did that. Called a friend, went someplace loud to drink and looked for a guy to pick up. Went to bed with him, no strings, no ridiculous exchange of names and phone numbers. Just bed.

Just sex.

Of course, some women did. They went looking for sex.

Sex with a stranger. A stranger with dark hair. Blue eyes. A square jaw, straight nose, firm mouth. And that little accent...

The phone rang. Let it. Her voice mail could take the call.

Hi, her recorded voice said briskly. *You've reached 555-6145. Please leave a message after the tone.*

"Aimee, it's Jen."

The last person she wanted to talk to! Jen had taken a job with Fox and Curtrain after Aimee pointed her toward it.

"I'm not going to take it," she'd said, "so why shouldn't you?"

Why, indeed?

"Aimee, look, I know this isn't your thing but a new club opened right near me and it's supposed to draw a hot crowd. And it's Laura's birthday, remember her, from the second floor in our dorm? She's in town and a bunch of us are getting together to, you know, check out the club..." There was giggling in the background and Aimee rolled her eyes. "Okay, Laura's right. To check out the guys, see if they're as hunky as everybody says."

"Jen?" Aimee said, picking up the phone.

"Oh, you're there! Listen, I don't know what you're doing tonight, but—"

"I'm not doing anything. I've had—it's been one of those days, you know?"

"All the more reason to go with us. Have a drink, listen to some hot music—"

"Get picked up by some hot guy," a female voice in the background said, to another round of giggles.

"That's the last thing I need," Aimee said. "I mean, is that all I'm good for? To go to a club where the music's so loud I won't be able to think? To let a guy pick me up, buy me a drink—"

"Yeah. I know. It's a meat market out there—but sometimes, well, sometimes that can be fun. You know. No BS. Just an evening of fun and games."

"It's bad enough men think that's what we're all about. That we're useless except in the kitchen or the bedroom. We don't have to play into their stupid fantasy."

Silence. Then Jen cleared her throat. "Okay," she said carefully, "so just forget that I—"

"Not that I couldn't be some jerk's idea of a centerfold playmate, if I wanted."

"Uh, Aimee, look, I have to run, so—"

"I could go to this club with you. Dance, drink, let some guy pick me up for a night of mind-blowing sex!"

The telephone line hummed with silence again. Then Jen spoke.

"So, uh, are you saying you want to go with us?"

Aimee took a deep, deep breath. "You're damned right I am," she said.

Twenty minutes later, dressed in a red silk dress she'd bought on sale and never had a reason to wear, ditto for a pair of strappy gold sandals, Aimee took a last look in the mirror, gave her image a quick salute, then headed out the door.

CHAPTER TWO

LUCAS'S CLUB was everything Damian had promised.

Like most hot Manhattan nightspots, it was in a neighborhood that had once been grungy and commercial and now was grungy and upscale. Streets that had once been relegated to the nitty-gritty of daily life now came alive after dark. Warehouses had given way to expensive, exclusive clubs.

Lucas's place was located in a dark brick building with shuttered windows. There was no sign to indicate that what had once been a factory was now Le Club Hot.

No sign. No published telephone number. You either knew the club existed or you didn't, which went a long way toward sorting out the clientele, Nicolo thought wryly as he opened a heavy, brass-hinged door and stepped, with Damian, into what might have been the small lobby of an upscale hotel.

The behemoth who greeted them was not someone you'd ever find behind a reception desk. They gave him their names, he checked a list, then smiled.

He pressed a button, and the wall ahead of them slid back.

"Wow," Damian said softly.

Nicolo had to agree. "Wow" summed it up.

The first thing you noticed was the noise. Music, heavy on bass, went straight into your blood.

Then you realized that the room you'd walked into was huge.

The designer had carefully left the exposed overhead pipes and old brick walls but everything else—the lighting, the endless Lucite bar, the elevated dance floor and the music—was dazzlingly modern.

"You could play American football in here," Damian murmured. "Especially since the place comes equipped with so many cheerleaders."

He grinned, and Nicolo grinned back at him. It was true. The room was filled with people, more than half of them women. Young. Stunning. Sexy. Faces recognizable from European and American magazine covers and movies.

What an idiot he'd been, letting what happened this afternoon get him worked up. Damian had it right. This was what he needed. Lights. Music.

Women.

This was the way to relax.

"Barbieri! Aristedes!"

Lucas was making his way through the crowd toward them. The men exchanged handshakes and then Lucas rolled his eyes and grabbed them both in a bear hug.

"Ugly as always," he said, raising his voice over the pulsating beat of the music, "but not to worry. I've told a bunch of lies about you both and made you sound so interesting that people are willing to meet you, despite your looks."

The three of them grinned. Then Lucas pointed toward a suspended, transparent staircase.

"My table's up there," he shouted. "On the mezzanine. It's quieter…and the view is *óptimo!*"

He was right. The table overlooked the dance floor and the sound level dropped from deafening to ear-shattering.

And the view was, indeed, excellent.

"What scenery," Damian said.

He meant, of course, the women. Nicolo nodded in agreement. He'd already acknowledged that the scenery was spectacular. All those lithe, gyrating bodies. The lovely faces…

Was there a woman on the dance floor with eyes the color of violets? With hair the honey-gold of a tigress?

"Nicolo? Which do you prefer?"

Nicolo blinked. Lucas and Damian were looking at him, along with a girl in gold hot pants and a skimpy black tank top.

"To drink," Lucas said, with a little laugh. "Whiskey? Champagne? The club special? It's a Mojito. You know, rum, lime juice—"

"Whiskey," Nicolo said, and told himself to stop being a fool and start having a good time.

But that was a problem.

It turned out you couldn't have a good time just by telling yourself to have one. You had to relax before you had fun, and now that the woman with the violet eyes had pushed her way into his head, he knew damned well "fun" wasn't going to happen.

No matter how much he tried.

He ate. He drank. He listened while Lucas and Damian caught up on old times. The three of them hadn't seen each other in months; there was a lot to talk about and he forced himself to join in the conversation.

After a while, his thoughts drifted. To the woman. To how he'd dealt with her. The more he thought, the angrier he became.

At her.

At himself.

What kind of man let a woman make a fool of him?

"Nicolo?"

Another blink, this time at Damian, who was watching him through slightly narrowed eyes.

"You okay?"

"Yes. Sure. I told you, it's—it's this meeting Monday, and—"

Lucas snorted. "My friend, you're as transparent as glass. What's on your mind is a woman."

No. It wasn't true. Well, yes. There was a woman on his mind but not in the way Lucas meant.

There were no women in his life to think about.

He'd ended an affair a month ago, and *grazie a Dio* that he had. The lady in question had been like so many others, beautiful and accommodating at first, then simply beautiful and boring.

But then, that was in the nature of things—or was it? Somehow, he couldn't envision the blonde with the violet eyes ever being accommodating or boring.

She would always be a challenge.

Any other woman, given the situation, would have accepted the apology he'd offered. Hell, any other woman would have done more than that.

He was always lucky with women. They liked him and he liked them. So, any other woman would have smiled and said it was nice of him to say it was his fault but, really, it was hers.

And he'd have understood her smile, returned one of his own and said, well, perhaps they might have a drink while they decided who owed whom an apology....

Nicolo brought his bourbon on the rocks to his lips and took a long drink.

Damn it, the woman was haunting him and for a reason that was insulting.

Such insolence! Why had he tolerated it? Such audacity! And he'd let her get away with it.

His eyes narrowed.

What she'd needed was a real lesson in how a woman should behave. Not that pale excuse of a kiss but something she would have remembered, something that would have shaken her loose of that cold disdain.

He should have dragged her against his body. Taken her mouth, parted her lips with his and filled her with his taste. Let her understand that she was female and he was male and despite the ridiculous conventions of this misbegotten century, what that meant was that he held supremacy when it came to things such as this.

But he had done none of those things. And now, for all he knew, somewhere in this vast city she was laughing at him. At how easily she'd cut him down to size.

Laughing, perhaps, with her lover.

A woman with a face like a madonna's would surely have a lover.

Would he be a man she could command? Yes. Of course. And what a pity that was because what the lady needed was a lover whose touch would make her tremble. Whose kisses would melt her icy hauteur. Who would make love to her until she begged for mercy…

"Barbieri!"

Nicolo forced the darkness away, looked at the expressions on his friends' faces—and realized that he had held his glass so tightly it had shattered.

Whiskey puddled on the table.

"Merda," he growled, and dabbed furiously at the spreading pond of golden liquid with a napkin.

"Never mind that. Did you cut yourself?"

Had he? Nicolo checked.

"No. Not a scratch." He forced a laugh and held out his hand. "See? Relax, Reyes. There won't be a lawsuit."

But Lucas wasn't buying into the poor attempt at humor.

"*Amigo,* I'm not the one who needs to relax. You're wound tighter than a spring."

Nicolo thought about denying it but what was the point? These men knew him too well.

"You're right. I am, and I'm sorry I'm spoiling your evening." He pushed back his chair. "The truth is, I can't keep my mind on things tonight, so I'm going to head back to my hotel. I told you, that meeting—"

"We've known you too long to fall for that. Tough negotiations don't stress you, Barbieri. You live for them." Laughing, Damian nudged Lucas in the ribs with his elbow. "It's a woman. Admit it."

Nicolo gave a deliberately careless shrug. Maybe if he made light of it…

"Okay," he said, "it is. But I'll get over it."

"Of course you will." Lucas leaned closer. "And I know the quickest way to do it. It's like drinking, Nicolo. Remember, back in college? The hair of the dog cure after too much partying? You wake with a hangover, you get rid of it by taking a drink. Well, you have a woman on the brain, you cure that by—"

"Lucas," a soft voice purred, "darling Lucas, here you are! We've been looking everywhere."

Five women had materialized beside the table. All stunning. All smiling as if they'd found the lost treasure of the Amazons.

"The hair of the dog, my man," Damian whispered, and Nicolo thought, *Why not?*

Chairs were dragged over. Introductions were made. Champagne corks popped. After a few minutes, one of the women—her name was Vicki—turned to Nicolo.

"Lucas tells me you're a royal"

Nicolo looked over her shoulder. Lucas grinned and winked.

"Lucas is a comedian," he said.

"I'm famous, too." She giggled. "Well, not yet but someday. Maybe you've seen me? I've been in—"

A list of plays. Or TV shows. Or something. He didn't know, didn't care, and stole a surreptitious glance at his watch. When could he get out of here without insulting the lady or putting a damper on the party?

Not that she wasn't beautiful. And friendly. She smiled a lot. Put her hand on his arm. Asked him the questions a man likes to be asked.

It was an old game, one he'd played often. The outcome was always understood. And pleasant.

Amazingly pleasant.

He felt his blood tingle. Damian was right. Lucas, too. This was what he needed. A willing, beautiful woman. A game with a predictable ending. A night's pleasure.

Wasn't it bad enough the woman with the violet eyes had made a fool of him once? Was he going to let her do it again by keeping him from what waited for him now?

Nicolo pushed back his chair. Took Vicki's hand.

"Dance with me."

He led her down the steps to the dance floor. Salsa music blasted the air, its insistent beat almost as sexual as the moves of Vicki's ripe body lightly brushing his.

Yes. This was good. This was what he needed…

But it wasn't. It was the wrong body, teasing his. The wrong face, lifted to his and smiling. The wrong eyes, filled with heat and desire.

Basta, he thought in disgust, and he put his arms around the woman and brought her tightly against him as the music segued into something slow and sexy.

She settled close against him as if she'd been waiting for the invitation. Her hair tickled his nose. It was stiff and smelled of hairspray.

Those honeyed curls this afternoon had been soft and fragrant with rain.

"It's terribly noisy here," Vicki said, her breath warm against his ear.

Why don't we find a quieter place? That was the next line. His, or in these days of supposed equality, it could be—

"Why don't we find a quieter place?" she whispered.

Nicolo cleared his throat.

"You know," he said, "I think that's—I think it's—" *An excellent idea.* "I think I'll have to take a rain check on that," he heard himself say.

She looked as surprised as he felt but, damn it, he didn't want this woman.

No substitutes, he thought as the music began to pound again, and the need, the desire he'd been suppressing all these hours ignited and threatened to consume him.

He knew what he wanted. What he needed. And there had to be a way, had to be something he could do to—

Nicolo caught his breath. He stopped dancing, let the other dancers and the music swirl around him.

There she was!

Honey-colored curls. Violet eyes. The woman who was driving him insane. No black suede coat. No hood. No boots. Instead she wore a clinging scrap of crimson silk that barely covered her body. Gold sandals, all straps and sky-high, needle-sharp heels. She was dancing, if you wanted to call it that. Moving in a man's arms. Breasts swaying. Hips rotating. Head up, eyes locked to the man's face, mouth turned up in a smile…

A smile she had denied him.

"Nicolo?"

Vicki, whatever her name was, said his name. Said something more and put her hand on his chest. He brushed it aside. Stepped away. Abandoned her in the middle of the crowded dance floor.

The part of his brain that was of this century knew all that. Knew, too, that his response to the events of the afternoon might not be entirely rational.

But the part that was as old, as savagely male, as time whispered, *This is what I want. And I'm going to have it.*

And Nicolo heard nothing else.

The music had turned wild; the throbbing pulse matched the insistent thump of his blood, the beat of his heart....

The fury eating inside him.

Fate, always capricious, had decided to favor him tonight. The woman who'd made a fool of him was here.

Now, he could even the score.

He shouldered his way through the crowd, eyes locked to his quarry. She was oblivious to him. Good, he thought grimly. He wanted to reach her before she had time to think.

But halfway there, she suddenly stopped dancing. Her partner said something; she didn't answer. Instead she moved out of his arms and stood like a doe at the edge of a clearing, sensing the presence of a hungry predator.

Later, Nicolo would wonder if it weren't the whole world that had gone still and waited, waited, waited.

A minute, an eternity, swept by. Then the blonde raised her head and looked directly at him.

He let a tight smile curve his mouth. Whatever beat its wings within him must have been in that smile, because the color drained from her face.

She took a step back.

He thought, again, of the doe.

Run, he thought.

And, just as if she'd read his mind, the woman with the violet eyes swung away from him and fled.

Nicolo didn't hesitate. He went after her.

CHAPTER THREE

You COULDN'T end up in the same place with the same man twice in one day. Not in a town the size of New York.

At first, when she saw him, Aimee told herself it had to be some other tall, dark-haired guy. There were tons of dark-haired, good-looking men in the city.

A second glance and that hope vanished. It was the overbearing, supermacho jerk who'd kissed her. It had to be. The truth was, nobody else would be as...

All right. No other man could possibly be as easy on the eyes. He was despicable—but he was gorgeous.

The last few minutes, she'd felt... What? A premonition? She didn't believe in any of that stuff, but how else to explain that tingle at her nape? That feeling that eyes were following her as she danced with Tom or Tim or, dear God, she couldn't even remember the name of the guy who'd bought her a drink, then led her onto the dance floor.

He was nice enough. Good-looking enough. And he was working hard at making an impression.

And he wasn't the stranger from this afternoon.

No way would Tom, or whoever he was, grab a woman and kiss her, look at her through icy deep-blue eyes in a way that would make the memory of him lodge itself in her brain.

She hated men like the Neanderthal, no matter how hot-looking a Neanderthal he might be.

So, yes, it was good that the guy dancing with her wasn't like that… Wasn't it?

Of course it was.

He'd been coming on to her like crazy. And she'd tried her best to respond. Smiled. Laughed. Gone onto the dance floor and did her best to lose herself in the music, working off her frustrations to its insistent beat the way she'd have worked them off in the gym.

And then, suddenly, she'd felt a tingle, as if someone was watching her.

Well, of course, someone was watching her! People danced, other people watched.

Aimee had danced harder, throwing herself into the music with abandon, and the guy with her kept saying things like, "Wow, you're good, baby," and "That's it, babe, way to go," as if he were cheering her on.

Objectifying her, she'd thought with detached clarity— except, wasn't that part of the deal tonight?

She'd come here to have fun, she'd thought grimly. To pick up a man. She was going to have a good time.

Except, she wasn't.

She despised places like this. Not the club itself: it was, she had to admit, spectacular. It was what went with the place. The noise. The lights. The crowd. The desperate pickup lines.

And this was not the time to turn into an anthropologist studying the natives.

So she'd agreed when Jen said it was absolutely fantastic, laughed at what she assumed were jokes, let a nice-looking guy buy her a margarita, tell her she was the most beautiful woman in the place and lead her to the dance floor.

And tried not to cringe each time Ted or Tim or Tom called her "baby."

And worked really, really hard at pretending she was having fun when the truth was, she didn't belong here, didn't want to be here, certainly didn't want to go home with Ted-Tom-Tim or anybody else for a night of meaningless sex.

She'd never treated sex casually. Never had a one-night stand. Never, not once.

Why on earth had she thought she'd want to now?

Because, a sly voice inside her had whispered, *you thought it just might make you forget the stranger. The one with the hard, beautiful face and the body that was all muscle.*

The one who kissed you as if he had the right, as if he could kiss you, do anything to you that he wanted.

That you *wanted.*

And that was when Aimee felt the tingling, looked around… And saw him. The stranger from this afternoon. Watching her with what could only be fury in his eyes.

He was angry? At *her?* That was crazy. *She* was the one who was angry. And "angry" wasn't the word. She'd been the one harassed by him. By his attitude. His arrogance. His unwanted kiss.

His eyes met hers. Everything faded. The insistent throb of the music, the people around her, everything.

Aimee stopped dancing.

It was all she could do not to run.

The look in his eyes terrified her…but the slow heat spreading through her veins terrified her even more.

She took a long, deep breath. Or tried to. For some reason, she couldn't seem to get any air into her lungs.

Suddenly the rage in his expression changed. Something else glittered in his dark blue eyes. Something male that she despised.

The innate male determination to dominate.

To dominate, in bed and out.

With breathtaking swiftness, she felt a rush of heat sweep through her. Her nipples tightened; a honeyed warmth spread low in her belly.

No, she thought frantically, no! She'd never want someone like him to put his hands on her. His mouth on her. To take her, hard and fast, again and again until she collapsed in his arms….

He started toward her, heedless of the people in his way, everything about him focused, with hot intensity, on her.

And she turned and ran.

She went through the crowd blindly, banging into people, ignoring their indignant protests. Her heart was racing.

God, oh God, oh God!

He was the hunter. She was his prey. A sob rose in her throat and, just in time, she spotted the flashing neon sign that marked one of the club's unisex bathrooms.

Jen had dragged her into it earlier.

"Doesn't look like a bathroom at all," Jen had bubbled.

Right now, it looked like a sanctuary.

Aimee pulled open the door. Slammed it after her. Started to turn the lock…

Bang!

The door flew open and the man burst into the room. She shrieked and fell back, reached behind her to the vanity. Wrapped her hand around a heavy bottle of something. Hand lotion. Body oil. Who gave a damn what it was? It was a weapon.

That was what counted.

"Don't," she said.

Her voice shook. Was that the reason for the little smile that began at the corner of his mouth?

"Get out of here! Do you hear me? Go away or I'll scream."

He laughed. She couldn't blame him. There wasn't a chance in the world anyone would hear her. You wouldn't hear a siren above the music. It was muted here, but it still filled the room like the beat of a giant heart.

She raised the bottle over her head. "One step," she panted, "just one, and I'll smash you with this!"

He laughed. "You already tried that, remember?"

"I'm not kidding! You—you unlock that door and get the hell out of here or so help me—"

He started toward her. She let fly with the bottle but he dodged and it shattered against the wall.

"Listen to me." Her voice trembled; she hated herself for it but she knew damned well there was nothing she could do to prevent it. "This is a terrible mistake. You won't—you won't get away with—"

"At first," he said, his tone almost conversational, "I thought, 'Well, that is just the way she deals with men.'"

She'd noticed his accent this afternoon. You couldn't miss that husky, sexy quality to his voice. It seemed more obvious now, his pronunciation more careful.

"I told myself it was not important."

Aimee swallowed. "Look, what happened this afternoon—"

"Still," he said, in that same easy way, as if he were explaining the day's news to a friend, "still, I admit, it bothered me. That a woman should be so impolite. So downright rude. But I put it out of my head."

"I didn't do anything! It was—it was just something that happened."

"Just something that happened." He nodded. "Yes, that's an excellent way to put it. In fact, that is exactly the conclusion I reached."

He was inches away from her now, so close that she had to tilt her head up to see his eyes. Even in her heels, he was much taller than she. And, God, much bigger.

"But then I saw you, here."

"You mean, you followed me here!"

"You give yourself too much importance, *cara*. Do you really think I have nothing better to do than to spend my time following you?" A little muscle was ticking in his cheek. "I came here with friends. To enjoy the evening." He paused. "And, it would seem, so did you."

"Yes. And—and my date will be looking for—"

"Your date didn't move a finger to prevent you from abandoning him. Or to keep me from going after you." He paused, and she saw his eyes darken. "I noticed that you treated your gentleman friend differently than you treated me."

"I don't know what you mean."

"*Cara.* Please, don't try my patience. You laughed with him. Smiled when he spoke to you."

"Of course. I mean, I know him—"

"Really? What's his name?"

"Ted," Aimee said quickly.

"No. It is not."

It had been a gamble, but a good one. Nicolo watched as the woman worried her bottom lip. He'd guessed right. She had no idea who she'd been dancing with. She'd picked the man up.

For many of its patrons, that was the purpose of a place like this.

Her business, of course.

That was what he'd told himself, when he first saw her with the man.

But he'd watched as she smiled. Flirted. Shook her hips, her breasts. Practiced the fine art of seduction.

For another man.

Not for him.

Not for him, he'd thought, and suddenly he'd known that confronting her, kissing her, would not be enough.

He wanted her.

It didn't make sense but it didn't have to. His body, his blood, knew what he needed.

And what he needed was this beautiful, condescending stranger dancing with him…

Dancing in his bed.

Slowly he reached out, laced one finger under the thin strap of her red dress and tugged. She stumbled toward him, arms raised, hands balled into fists.

He caught her wrists in one hand.

"Don't struggle," he said in a low voice. "It will only make things worse."

"Please." Her voice trembled. "Please, don't do this."

"I told you this afternoon, you lack manners, *cara*."

"Let me go! Damn you—"

"The next time 'something happens,' as you called it, between you and a man, you will know how to respond."

"If you're after an apology…"

"And if I were, would you finally offer one?"

She was terrified; he could see it in her face, feel it in the trembling of her body. Her gaze locked on his, and he felt a rush of disappointment.

She was desperate, desperate enough so she was, in fact, going to apologize. And then, as a civilized man, he'd have to let her go…

Wrong.

Her chin lifted; terrified or not, her eyes blazed with defiance.

"Only a barbarian would think that taking a woman by force is the way to get even for damage to his ego."

"Is that what you think? That I'm going to rape you?" The muscle flickered in his jaw again; he cupped her face with his free hand and held it steady. "You know better." His voice was low and husky. "I saw the way you looked at me a few minutes ago."

Color stained her cheeks. "I don't know what you—"

"Yes," he said, "you damned well do."

His head lowered to hers, and he kissed her.

His mouth was hard. Hungry. Hot against hers. Aimee jerked against the restraint of his hand, tried to twist her face away but he wouldn't permit it.

Instead he brought her closer, crushing her tightly against him so that she could feel the strength of him, the power....

The thrust of his straining erection.

A whimper rose in her throat.

"Stop," she said, against his mouth, but he went on kissing her, his fingers sliding into her hair, twisting the curls around his hand, backing her against the wall so that now she was pressed against him from breast to groin.

"Kiss me back," he said in a thick whisper.

No, she told herself frantically. She wouldn't. She wouldn't. She wouldn't...

Aimee gave a strangled cry, rose to him and opened her mouth against his.

He groaned. Let go of her wrists and threw his arm around her hips, lifting her against him. His tongue teased her lips, slipped between them and she tasted his hunger, his need, his rampant masculinity.

"Say it," he growled against her mouth. "Tell me what you want. What you've wanted ever since this afternoon."

Blind to logic, to reason, blind to anything but the feel of him, the scent of him, Aimee gave up lying.

"You," she whispered. "Only you. All day. All evening. I couldn't think of anything else, couldn't get you out of my head—"

He cupped her face in his hands. Kissed her, deeply. Thrust his leg between hers and she moaned at the feel of it against the tender flesh between her thighs.

She moved against him. Moved again, but it wasn't enough, wasn't enough…

She moaned.

The sound damned near sent Nicolo over the edge.

The taste of her was exquisite. She was strawberries and cream, spring rain and summer sun. She was everything a man could imagine a woman might be, if only in a dream.

He lifted her from the floor. Her arms rose; she wound them around his neck.

"Yes," he said, and he grasped her slender thighs and brought them around his hips.

He thought of taking her to his hotel. To her apartment. To a place where he could undress her, touch her, watch her eyes as he entered her.

But not now.

Now, he needed this. Needed her. Needed to bury himself in her, needed it more than his next breath.

Locked in a dance as old as time, mouths fused in mutual hunger, Nicolo carried Aimee to the marble vanity. Sat her on its edge. Fumbled between them. Unzipped. Freed himself. Put his hand between her thighs, groaning as he felt the wet heat of her against his fingers, and tore aside the scrap of silk that kept her from him.

"Look at me," he commanded.

She did, fixing those incredible violet eyes on his face.

"Yes," she said, and he thrust forward, sank into her, felt her close around him.

She cried out instantly; he felt the pulse of her muscles

as she came and then he exploded within her, came in a rush of almost unbearable ecstasy.

She trembled.

Then she gave a little sob and dropped her head on his shoulder.

Nicolo put his arms around her. Stroked her silken hair. Whispered to her, his native language soft on his tongue while he tried to figure out what in hell had just happened.

This was not the first time he'd had quick, hot sex. It was not the first time he'd had sex in the hidden heart of a public place.

Both could be exciting.

The truth was, sex was always exciting. But this, what had just happened... He'd never experienced anything like it.

He didn't even know this woman's name.

He hadn't used a condom.

Madre del dio, was he losing his mind?

And then she sighed. Her breath tickled his throat. She lifted her head and looked at him, her eyes filled with uncertainty, her mouth gently swollen from his kisses, and Nicolo forgot everything but the soft, sweet feel of her mouth, her arms, her thighs.

"I don't—I don't know what happened." Her voice was shaky, her face white except for two spots of color high on her cheeks. "I never—God, I never—"

"No. Nor have I."

She started to speak again and he knew what she would say, that this was wrong, that he had to let her go.

He knew of only one way to keep her from saying those words.

He kissed her.

Gently at first but then—then, the fierce wave of desire swept over him. And over her. He felt her swift intake of breath, the whispered plea against his lips, and suddenly he was deep inside her again, rocking against her, swallowing her cries, coming when she came and knowing that it still wasn't enough, that he needed more....

Someone pounded on the locked door.

The woman in his arms blanched.

"It's all right," he whispered, but she shook her head.

"No. Someone's outside. They'll see—"

He brushed his lips over hers. Then he set her on her feet and did what needed to be done to make himself presentable. She did the same, but he saw that her hands were shaking.

"*Cara.* Don't be—"

"Hey, you gonna be in there all night?"

Nicolo looked down into the face of the woman he'd just made love to. "It's time we introduced ourselves," he said softly. "My name is—"

She put her palm over his mouth. "No. No names. This was—it was only a dream."

He caught her hand, pressed his lips to it, then closed her fingers over the kiss.

"A dream. *Si.* And there is no need for the dream to end so soon."

"No. I can't. I—"

"We can," he said fiercely. "We can do anything, if this is a dream."

She shook her head but he drew her into his arms and kissed her, telling her without words how it could be between them, how it would be when they had all the time and privacy they needed.

Her lips softened. Clung to his. She sighed, and he cupped her face with his hands.

"Come with me," he whispered.

She shook her head again; he kissed her again.

"Is there another man?"

"No," she said quickly. "But—"

"We're adults, *cara*. Both of us are free. Come with me. Be with me tonight."

He kissed her and the world spun around them. Then he lifted his head and looked down into her eyes.

"Yes," she said softly.

Nicolo felt his heart soar. He encircled her waist with his arm, drew her against him, led her to the door and unlocked it.

A man was waiting outside.

"It's about time. I mean, how long did you…" His gaze fell on Aimee and he raised his eyebrows. "Oh. I get it. Hey, no problem. I had a babe like this with me, I'd—"

"Watch your mouth," Nicolo said, his voice cold and flat.

The man's face went pale. He stepped out of their way. And Aimee thought, *What am I doing?*

She'd just had sex with a stranger. A stranger she knew nothing about, except that he could be hard and cold and terrifying….

Her nameless lover drew her close. "Don't think," he said, as if he'd read her mind. "Not tonight."

She looked up at him, into those blue eyes that could go from winter ice to summer sun. Remembered the feel of his hands on her. The feel of him in her, and let the last vestige of sanity slip away.

There was a taxi at the curb. It took them uptown, to a hotel on the park.

He had a suite. It was huge. Luxurious.

Was money a good character reference? she thought, and would have laughed but he was taking her into his arms, slipping the straps of her dress from her shoulders. Cupping her breasts, tasting them, ohgod,ohgod,ohgod…

The hours after that were a blur of excitement. Of whispers and sighs and explorations. Aimee lost herself in a sea of sensation....

And shot awake in the gray hours before dawn, suddenly aware that she was wrapped in the embrace of a man she didn't know.

A hot tide of shame engulfed her.

Trembling, she disentangled herself from the possessive curve of his arm. Dressed in the dark, slipped from the sumptuous suite and sneaked down the service staircase because the thought of facing the elevator operator made her feel ill.

Moments later, Nicolo came awake and reached for his lover.

The bed, the sitting room, the bathroom were empty.

He cursed, pulled on trousers and shirt, hurried out into the corridor, but she was gone. He rang for the elevator. No, the operator said, he hadn't taken anyone down to the lobby.

He went to the reception desk, demanded to know if the clerk had seen a woman with honey-blond hair and violet eyes. The answer there was the same.

She had vanished.

As the sun rose over the city, Nicolo paced his rooms while he tried to figure out how in hell he would find a nameless woman in a city of eight million people.

The one certainty was that he would find her.

Nicolo Barbieri did not believe in defeat.

By Sunday evening, Nicolo had learned an ugly lesson.

A man didn't have to believe in defeat to be subjected to it.

You couldn't find a woman without a name, not even if you slipped hundred-dollar bills to the club's bouncer and all its bartenders.

They all said the same thing. Lots of women came through the doors on a Saturday night. So what if one had hair the color of honey and eyes the color of violets? That didn't mean much to them.

All right, Nicolo told himself coldly.

It didn't meant much to him, either.

A woman had let him pick her up and take her to bed. She'd probably done the same thing dozens of times before. So what if he never saw her again? All that bothered him was that she'd slipped from his arms without a word.

It didn't, *she* didn't, mean a thing.

He told himself that as he showered Monday morning. Told himself, too, all that mattered was what had brought him to New York. The meeting at SCB with James Black. The acquisition of the old man's kingdom. Nothing was as important as—

The phone rang.

Nicolo flung open the shower door and grabbed for the receiver.

The woman. It had to be.

But it wasn't. It was Black's secretary, calling to cancel the meeting. Black was indisposed. The secretary would be in touch when he was available again.

Nicolo said all the right things. Then he hung up the phone and stared blindly at the mirror over the vanity.

Was it true? Or had Black simply decided not to see him? The old man had a reputation. He liked to treat people like marionettes.

The woman with the violet eyes was the same. She seduced a man, gave him a few hours' taste of what it was like to possess her and then she slipped away.

Nicolo's hands knotted into fists.

Black would pay by selling him SCB. As for the

woman… She would pay, too. Somehow, he would find her and teach her what it meant to walk out on him.

He was as certain of that as he was of his next breath.

CHAPTER FOUR

SUMMER had finally arrived.

No more chilly wind and soaking rain. Instead the city was wrapped in soft breezes and warm sunshine.

The weather was so spectacular that even New Yorkers smiled at each other.

Aimee didn't notice.

Memories of what she'd done, that she'd gone to bed with a stranger, haunted her, intruded when she least expected.

Walking down the street, she'd turn a corner and see a tall, broad-shouldered man with dark hair and her heart would skip a beat.

Or she'd be in bed, asleep, and suddenly he'd materialize in her dreams.

She'd see his beautiful, hard face. His powerful body. And he'd touch her, kiss her, do things to her no one had ever done, make her feel things she'd never felt....

Until one night in a stranger's arms.

She tried not to think about that because it seemed so wrong. Still, in her sleep, she'd moan at his touch and awake, shaken and breathless, her skin hot, her body aching for his possession even though her conscious mind knew she despised him, despised herself....

No. It was not turning out to be a good summer, she

thought as she stepped from the shower on a balmy June morning. The man. The ugliness of what she'd done.

Then, that same weekend, her grandfather's stroke.

Her mouth tightened.

Good old Bradley had rushed to the rescue. By the time she reached the hospital, her cousin was there with two of his SCB cronies. He had a piece of paper in his hand, James's signature scrawled across it.

Something that he and his pals swore was James's signature, anyway.

"Uncle has made me his surrogate until he recovers," he'd told her with ill-concealed triumph.

Aimee tossed aside her bath towel and went to the closet.

She should have fought him. Hired an attorney. But she'd felt such despair that Sunday, such self-loathing, that fighting Bradley was the last thing she'd wanted to do.

Bradley settled into James's office and immediately began making decisions that left her reeling, but there was nothing she could do. He was in charge until Grandfather recovered. She'd thought of going directly to James, but she had no way of knowing what condition he was in. He was in seclusion at his home, surrounded by doctors, nurses and therapists, and supposedly had left strict orders that he did not want to see visitors.

Hands tied, Aimee had only been able to wait. And wonder.

Yesterday, the waiting had ended.

James's secretary—Bradley's secretary, now—had phoned and told her she was expected at Stafford-Coleridge-Black promptly at ten this morning.

"I'm sorry, Miss Black," the woman said crisply when Aimee started to ask questions. "I can't tell you anything except to assure you that you'll have all the answers tomorrow."

As if she needed them, Aimee thought bitterly. She knew exactly what would happen this morning. Her cousin, seated behind James's imposing desk, would flash his oily smile and tell her he was in charge, permanently.

She'd fight him, of course, just on principle. But she'd lose. Bradley had that document and witnesses. She had nothing—certainly not the money for a protracted court battle.

Lately she didn't even have the energy.

She was tired all the time. Exhausted, really. Plagued by bouts of nausea.

Stress, she'd told herself. Over her grandfather because, despite everything, he was her blood and she loved him. Over what would become of Stafford-Coleridge-Black, because she loved it, too.

And stress over that night. What she'd done. That she'd let a stranger seduce her—

Except, he hadn't. She'd gone to him willingly. Eagerly. Making love with him was the most exciting thing she'd ever done. Sex had never been like that before. Sex would never be like that again, especially since she couldn't imagine being with another man....

Aimee blinked.

She had more important things on her mind this morning.

Yesterday, she'd finally gone to her doctor for a checkup. He'd listened to her litany of complaints, examined her, had his nurse take blood and urine samples and told her he'd have lab reports in a few days.

"Not to worry, Ms. Black," he'd said briskly. "I suspect whatever ails you is simple to deal with."

Vitamins, she'd thought. More rest.

Fewer dreams.

Still, it was hard not to worry until the lab results were in and now, on top of everything else, she had this meeting Bradley had orchestrated, undoubtedly so he could crow with triumph as he told he'd taken permanent control of the reins.

When she was dressed—cotton summer suit, low heels, light makeup—Aimee looked in the mirror. The woman looking back at her was the woman she really was. Intelligent. Educated. Competent.

She bore no resemblance to the woman in the bathroom mirror that night at the club…

No. She would not let those memories take over this morning.

Bradley was about to knife her in the back, but she'd be damned if she'd let him see her bleed.

She would show absolutely no emotion today, no matter what happened.

That was the plan, and it would have worked…except for what she found waiting for her in the Stafford-Coleridge-Black boardroom.

Grandfather, not Bradley, sat ramrod-straight in his usual chair at one end of the long mahogany conference table.

The stranger she'd gone to bed with was seated at the other.

Nicolo was not in a good mood.

He was in New York for the first time since the episode three months before and he'd found the night had tainted his feelings about the city.

Unfortunate.

He'd always enjoyed spending time in Manhattan. Now, he couldn't wait to see the last of it. And, he thought, with a not-so-discreet glance at his Tag Heuer watch as he sat waiting for the meeting in James Black's office to begin, he would be doing that soon.

Just this one last session with Black and the deal he and the old man had worked on the past two weeks, via a volley of faxes and phone calls, would be completed.

Yesterday, when they'd met face-to-face, Black told him there was just one last point to agree upon.

"Just one," he'd repeated, his voice quavering because of the stroke that had, it was said, almost killed him.

"And that is?" Nicolo had replied.

Black had wagged a bony finger. "Nothing a smart man won't be willing to accede to, Prince Barbieri, I assure you."

Nicolo had almost reminded him that he didn't use his title, but he'd decided to play along. Black obviously liked the idea that Nicolo was royalty. Why do anything to spoil the finalization of the deal?

Not that he was concerned over this last point, especially since he was sure he knew what it was. They'd agreed on a price. On a takeover date. What could be left to discuss?

Only Black's repeated concern that the company his ancestors had founded not lose its identity among Nicolo's holdings.

The old man, he was sure, was going to want some sort of guarantee, and Nicolo had come up with one.

He would keep the bank's name, Stafford-Coleridge-Black, intact.

In fact, he'd almost said so yesterday in hopes of avoiding this morning's meeting, but he suspected that giving in without at least a small battle would only make Black ask for something more.

So he'd agreed to today's meeting, which had meant spending another night in the city.

Another night plagued by memories of how he'd let a woman make a fool of him.

Dio, how ridiculous he was! He'd had a night of sex—the best sex of his life, and that was saying a great deal. A night of fantastic sex, with no morning-after to deal with. No female batting her lashes over coffee, telling him how wonderful he was, asking when she would see him again.

Ask half a dozen men what was wrong with that scenario and they'd laugh and say there wasn't a thing wrong with it.

Mind-blowing sex. No names. No commitment. A man's fantasy.

Then why was it driving him insane, that she'd left his bed while he slept? Why should it bother him?

He still winced when he recalled how he'd gone searching for her in the hall. Made a fool of himself with the elevator operator, the night clerk. Taken a cab to that damned club and demanded answers.

Embarrassing? A little…

Hell. A lot.

A woman should not be the one who walked out of a relationship. Even if that "relationship" only lasted a few hours. Yes, he knew all about the Age of Equality but a woman had never walked out on him, not under any circumstances.

This one had, and he didn't like it.

That was why she was in his head, even now. Even when he was about to complete a deal he'd worked on, dreamed of, for years. Instead of concentrating on it, he was thinking about a woman who—

"Prince Barbieri?"

Who should consider herself fortunate he'd had no way to locate her because if he had—

"Prince Barbieri. Sir? If you please—"

"Si," Nicolo said, and cleared his throat. "Are you ready to begin? I was, ah, I was just reading through my notes, and—"

And, he looked up.

The world tilted.

The woman with the violet eyes was standing in the doorway staring at him just as he was staring at her, as if one of them was an apparition.

He saw the color drain from her face. Saw her mouth drop open. Saw the swift rise and fall of her breasts beneath the jacket of a demure blue suit.

"Demure" was the word for her, all right. Whoever she was, whatever she was doing here, today she was playing the part of a virgin.

A muscle knotted in Nicolo's jaw.

He shoved back his chair. Rose to his feet, his eyes never leaving her. She took a quick step back. Her lips formed a silent plea.

No!

He forgot everything. The boardroom. The old man. The deal he'd worked so long to finalize.

"Yes," he said grimly. "Oh, most definitely yes, *cara!*"

She shook her head. Stumbled back another step...

"Do you two know each other?" Black asked.

Nicolo swung his head toward the old man. "What?"

"I said, have you met my granddaughter before, Your Highness?"

Nicolo, a man who had glibly talked his way into the presence of captains of industry and heads of nations during his determined rise to the top, opened his mouth, then shut it again.

Black's granddaughter? This—this creature who would sleep with a stranger and then disappear into the night was his granddaughter?

Yes. Of course. A spoiled rich brat, accustomed to playing a seductive nymph by night and a sweet virgin by day. He'd seen lots of women like this. The rich seemed to specialize in breeding them.

"Grandfather." Her voice shook but Nicolo had to give her credit for recovering fast. "I—I didn't realize you were busy. I'll come back later. This afternoon. Or tomorrow. Or—"

"Prince Barbieri? Please, sit down. You, too, Aimee. This meeting very much concerns you."

Her stricken gaze swept from the old man to Nicolo.

Nicolo narrowed his eyes. What the hell was going on here? The temptation to tell Black he would not talk business in front of the woman was strong, but he suspected Black would not back down. He wanted her here, but why?

Nicolo had no choice but to learn why.

"What a pleasant surprise," he said, his tone silken, "Miss… Is it Miss Black?"

She nodded. "That's—that's correct."

"Ah. In that case, please, join us."

The look she gave him told him she'd regained her composure.

"My grandfather's already asked me to stay. I don't need your invitation."

"Aimee!"

"No. That's all right, Signore Black." Nicolo drew his lips back in a cold smile. "Your granddaughter is right. These are your offices, not mine."

"But not for long," the old man said.

Aimee looked at him. "What does that mean?"

"Sit down, Aimee, and you'll find out."

Nicolo pulled out the chair beside his. "An excellent suggestion, Miss Black." His voice hardened. "Sit down."

He saw her throat move as she swallowed. Then she raised her chin, ignored him and took the seat to the right of her grandfather. Nicolo sat down, too, and Black cleared his throat.

"Well," he said briskly, "you haven't answered my question. Do you know each other?"

"We—we might have met before," Aimee said.

"Have we?" Nicolo flashed another icy smile. "Perhaps your memory is better than mine. After all, if we'd met, we'd know each other's names, wouldn't we?"

Color painted crimson patches on her cheeks but when she spoke, her tone was cool.

"I really don't see that it matters." She turned to her grandfather. "Who is this man? And why is he here?"

Black folded his gnarled hands on the highly polished wood before him.

"Aimee, this is Nicolo Barbieri. Prince Nicolo Barbieri, of Rome."

Her expression showed how little impressed she was by his title.

"I suppose you expected to find Bradley." Black glanced at Nicolo. "My nephew and Aimee's cousin."

Aimee didn't answer. She was stunned by the presence of the stranger she'd slept with. Why was he here? And what was he going to say about that night?

"Aren't you curious as to why Bradley isn't present, Aimee?"

A good question. Bradley would never miss the chance to see her reaction as control of SCB was placed permanently in his hands.

Aimee sat up straight. Finding this—this man here had driven logical thought out of her head and she could not let that happen, not if there was the slightest chance of talking sense to her grandfather.

"I am curious," she said. "Knowing Bradley, I'd assume he'd want to be here to gloat."

James chuckled. "As you can see," he told Nicolo, "my granddaughter believes in being frank." He turned his attention to Aimee. "But Bradley has nothing to gloat about. I am, as you can see, in control of things again and after examining the records of the past three months, I can see that I was wrong to put Bradley in charge."

Aimee put her hands in her lap and clenched them into fists.

"I'm glad you realize that, Grandfather."

James nodded. "It's the reason you're here today."

"Excuse me," Nicolo said with barely concealed impatience, "but I would like to be let in on what is happening here, Signore Black. What has this woman—"

"My granddaughter. My own flesh and blood."

"What has she to do with our agreement?"

"What agreement?" Aimee said, looking from her grandfather to Nicolo.

"Aimee believes she should take over as head of Stafford-Coleridge-Black, Prince Barbieri."

Nicolo's mouth twitched. A woman, *this* woman, in charge of a private bank worth billions? He would have laughed, but the old man's expression was serious.

At least now he understood why Aimee Black was in the room. Her grandfather wanted her present for the announcement of his decision to sell the bank to Nicolo. Was it because he thought she'd take the news better than hearing it another way? Was it because Black thought, as he did, that her hope to head SCB was laughable?

Nicolo didn't give a damn.

For weeks, he'd imagined all the ways in which he could get even with this woman but what was about to happen was better than anything he'd considered. Her shock when she learned that he, of all people, was going to get what she so obviously—so foolishly—wanted, was more than he could have hoped for.

Sometimes, he thought, sitting back in his chair, sometimes, a man got very, very lucky.

"My granddaughter worked here summers for many years."

"How nice," Nicolo purred.

"She studied finance, economics and business."

Nicolo tried to look impressed. Amazing, what they taught rich girls in boarding school these days.

"She knows how I felt about keeping SCB in the family."

Nicolo nodded. "Unfortunately," he said politely, "fate did not cooperate."

"No. Not until now."

Nicolo frowned. Even a prince could smell a rat when it got close enough. "I'm afraid I don't understand, Signore Black."

James looked at Aimee. "How badly do you want to keep Stafford-Coleridge-Black in our family?" he said softly.

Aimee's heart began to race. "You know the answer to that, Grandfather."

"Now, just a moment, Black." Nicolo sat forward, his eyes narrowed and fixed on the old man's face. "We have a deal."

"What deal?" Aimee said.

"We have a tentative agreement, Prince Barbieri. Subject, as you know, to the outcome of this meeting."

"I do not like being hustled," Nicolo said sharply.

"Hustled?"

"Hustled. Played for a fool. Pushed for more money."

"This is not about money, Your Highness."

"*Dio,* will you stop calling me that? Call me by my last name. My first name. Just stop with the nonsense." Nicolo slapped his hand on the table. "Damn it, just tell me what you want."

James took a long breath.

"I want this institution to be in the hands of someone

with experience. Someone with a record of achievement that I can trust."

"That someone is me," Nicolo said coldly, "and we both know it."

"I also want it to be the legacy I leave to future generations of Blacks. Call it pride, call it what you will, Barbieri, but I don't wish to see two hundred years disappear."

"I understand." Nicolo took a breath, too. For a couple of minutes, he'd thought the old man was trying to tell him the sale was off. Impossible, of course. Black was not a sentimentalist. He would never leave the bank in the hands of an irresponsible female. "And that is why I'm sure what I say next will please you, *signore*. I've decided to retain the name of the bank. It will be known as Stafford-Coleridge-Black, just as it has for generations."

Aimee snorted. Nicolo shot her a warning look.

"Do you find this amusing, *signorina?*"

"I find it arrogant, *signore*. Can you actually believe my grandfather is naïve enough to think you've decided to keep a name that's worth its weight in gold in financial circles as an act of kindness?"

Nicolo gave her a long, cold look. Then he turned to James.

"With all due respect," he said, in a tone that made it clear the words were a polite lie, "I will not continue this meeting with your granddaughter present."

"With all due respect," Aimee snapped, "*you* are the outsider here, Prince Barbieri."

"You know nothing about this."

"I know everything about it."

Nicolo's mouth thinned. "What you know," he said slowly, "has nothing to do with boardrooms or corporations or responsibility. The only person here who does not know that is your grandfather."

Aimee sprang to her feet. "You—you no good, insolent son of a—"

"Stop it!" James's voice was sharp. "Aimee. You are to show the prince respect."

"Respect? If you knew—if you only knew what this man is really like. If you knew the truth about him—"

"Tell him," Nicolo said softly. "Go on, Miss Black. Why not explain things to your grandfather?"

Aimee stared at him, eyes glittering with angry tears, lips pouting with suppressed rage, breasts rising and falling with each breath.

It made him remember how she had looked that night, in his arms.

In his bed.

With a swiftness that stunned him, he felt his body harden.

"Why is he here?" she said, her voice rising. "I demand to know the reason!"

James Black looked from his granddaughter to the one man he was certain could guide the company he loved through the twenty-first century. Bradley couldn't do it. Aimee had tried to make him see that, and she'd been right. In the short time the boy had been at the helm, the company had lost clients and come close to taking dangerous changes of direction.

That left only one other Black to head the bank.

Aimee.

In the endless weeks of his recuperation, James had finally reviewed the proposals she'd made and he'd ignored. They were, he'd been forced to admit, good.

Excellent, actually.

And Aimee was of his blood.

But she was also a woman. A young woman. Even if he managed to convince himself that her sex was not a drawback, her inexperience was.

How could he entrust her with the responsibility handed down by generations of Staffords, Coleridges and Blacks?

He'd put thoughts of Aimee aside. Concentrated on Nicolo Barbieri. The man had the intelligence, the courage, the experience to move SCB forward.

If only he carried the right blood, James had thought…

And the solution had come to him.

Barbieri was young. Thirty, thirty-two. Something like that. Aimee was in her midtwenties.

Once upon a time, nations had forged bonds through marriage. So had powerful institutions. Men and women had been joined in matrimony so they could produce children who carried the proud ancestry of both.

"Grandfather, I want an answer. Why is Nicolo Barbieri here?"

Black looked at the Italian prince, then at his headstrong American granddaughter.

"He is here," he said calmly, "to make you his wife."

CHAPTER FIVE

FOR A MOMENT, no one spoke. No one moved. Even the dust motes hovered in the silence.

Then Aimee collapsed into her chair and made a choked sound. Was she laughing? One glance at her and Nicolo knew she wasn't. She looked the way he felt, as if an elephant had suddenly appeared in their midst.

"A bad joke, Grandfather. Now tell me the real reason."

"That is the real reason." James was unsmiling as he met her eyes. "You have some good ideas, Aimee, but you're too inexperienced to run SCB."

"I'm fully capable of running SCB. And in the event I needed advice, I'd turn to you."

"If I could rely on lasting long enough to do that," her grandfather said bluntly, "I wouldn't be handing my company to someone else."

"I'm not someone else. I'm your granddaughter!"

"You need guidance, Aimee." The old man paused. "And you need a husband. A woman's function is to marry and bear children."

Fascinated, not yet believing what was happening, Nicolo sat back and became a silent observer.

"You're a century behind the times, Grandfather."

"So it would seem. Which is why I'm willing to see

you as second-in-command to a man capable of running my company."

"Second-in-command?" Aimee's voice rose. "Do you actually think I'd agree to such an arrangement?"

"Stafford-Coleridge-Black needs strong, proven leadership. It also needs, as you have pointed out many times, new blood. His Highness can provide both those things." Black fixed her with an autocratic eye. "He can also provide our bank with a new generation of leaders."

A flush rose in her cheeks. "You speak as if—as if I'm a broodmare!"

"I speak sense, child," Black said, somewhat more gently. "You know I do. This is the perfect solution to everything."

A muscle knotted in Nicolo's jaw as silence fell over the room again. The offhand comment about providing the bank with a new generation was, perhaps, the most infuriating of all the infuriating things the old man had said.

If he took Aimee Black to bed, breeding a future generation of bankers would not be the reason.

What about the night you spent with her, Nicolo? A man who doesn't use a condom is a man flirting with fatherhood.

A knot formed in his belly. He'd never done such a foolhardy thing before, forgotten protection in the rush to take a woman, but then, he'd never done anything as crazy as making love to a stranger, either.

He looked at Aimee.

Nothing to worry about, he thought coldly. A woman who slept with a nameless man would be using protection of her own. She looked innocent now, in that demure outfit, tears glittering in her eyes, but it was all an act.

An act, he thought, and felt anger overtake surprise. What a pair they were, the old man and his granddaughter.

Did they really take him for such an easy mark?

Perhaps it was time to remind them of who he was.

"Excuse me," he said, his voice dangerously soft, "but perhaps I might say a word… Or would that spoil this rather amusing little scene?"

"Your Highness." James Black cleared his throat. "Maybe I should have mentioned this to you during an earlier meeting, but—"

"Indeed, *signore*. Maybe you should have."

"I considered it, but—"

"But, you were afraid I'd laugh in your face."

"I admit, I thought it possible you might see my idea as…unpalatable."

The woman gave a soft moan, as if she'd only just remembered his presence. Nicely timed, Nicolo thought, and decided the game had gone on long enough.

"There is more than that possibility," he said coldly, as he pushed back his chair. "There is that certainty."

"Your Highness—"

"Yes," Nicolo said through clenched teeth, "that is who I am. I am Prince Nicolo Antonius Barbieri, of a lineage much older and far more honorable than yours, and you would do well to remember it."

Had he really said that? *Dio,* he had. And his speech was going from lightly accented to the way it had been when he'd first come to this country to attend university, thirteen years ago.

It was a measure of his rage, and rage was not a good thing. A man could only succeed when his emotions were under control.

Nicolo stood and wrapped his hands tightly around the top rung of his chair.

"You were right, Signore Black. I would have brought this bank the leadership it needs. And, someday, I will surely produce the sons who will succeed me." He flashed a look at Aimee, whose cheeks were crimson.

Good, he thought with savage pleasure. It was a joy to see her humiliated.

"But I will do that with a woman of my choosing, who brings pride to my name and not dishonor."

Aimee's chair fell back as she scrambled to her feet and rounded the table to face him, head high, lips drawn back in a snarl.

"You—you no good, dissolute son of a bitch!"

"*I* am dissolute?" Nicolo let go of the chair and pounded his fist on the table. So much for self-control. "No, Miss Black. I hardly think it's *I* who should bear that label."

"You think, because you're a man, you can keep to a different level of morality? Let me tell you something, Prince Whoever You Are—"

"Do not think to lecture *me* about morals, Miss Black. Not unless you want me to tell your grandfather about the night we spent together." He paused, and his mouth twisted. "Or does he already know the salient details?"

All the color drained from her face. "What?"

"Your grandfather gives as good a performance as you. Not quite as enjoyable as the one you gave this spring, but still more than acceptable."

James looked from one of them to the other. "I'm afraid I don't understand."

"Of course you understand." Nicolo gathered his papers together and stuffed them into his briefcase. "I am Italian. My people go back to the time of Caesar. My bloodlines flow with conspiracy."

"What conspiracy?" Black sputtered.

"Which of you planned this?" A smile slashed across his face. "No matter. It comes to the same thing—though

I admit, I choose to believe the added touch of seduction was the lady's idea."

"Don't," Aimee said, reaching out her hand. "I beg you. Don't say anymore."

"She and I would meet, seemingly by accident. I would find her coldness enticing."

"Aimee? What is he talking about?"

"Then the sex. Incredible sex, but then, nothing less would do. And the coup de grâce. The disappearing act and the hope that I'd want more of what I had that night, enough so that when I learned the identity of my seductress, this little melodrama could be played for its full impact." He looked at Aimee. "That was a nice touch, by the way, that 'I'd never marry this man' routine. My compliments. If I hadn't known better, I'd have believed it."

Her eyes, the color of pansies in the rain, pleaded with him to stop.

For one brief moment, he remembered how terrified she'd been when he followed her into the bathroom at Lucas's club. How worried that someone would see them.

And he remembered what he had not permitted himself to remember until now, the way she'd trembled when he took her to his bed, the way she'd looked up at him when he made love to her, really made love to her, kissing her slowly, savoring her taste, taking all the time in the world to caress her and stroke her and, at last, enter her, how her face, her whispers, her caresses had told him that what she was feeling, what he was making her feel, was new and incredible and had never happened to her before.

Liar, Nicolo thought, and anger became rage so fierce it slammed into him like a fist.

"Wasted effort," he said roughly. "You understand, Black? I'm not interested in you or your bank or your slut of a granddaughter."

Aimee whipped her hand through the air and slammed it against his jaw. Nicolo grabbed her wrist and put enough pressure on it to make her yelp.

"Don't," he said, his voice soft with malice. "Do you hear me? Don't do anything you will regret."

"I couldn't regret anything more than being with you that horrid night!"

She was shaking now, her eyes glistening with hatred for him. That was fine. Let her hate him. God knew, he hated her and the despicable old man who sat watching them.

James Black was sick, all right, but it had nothing to do with his stroke. His sickness was moral depravity.

The old man loved his damnable bank more than his granddaughter, who he'd sent to seduce him.

The night had been a travesty of passion. All of it. The deep kisses. The sighs. The way she'd framed his face with her hands and brought his mouth to hers while her dark-gold hair spread in abandon over his pillow.

Cursing, Nicolo reached for her now, dragged her to her toes and crushed her mouth beneath his. She cried out and it only made him more furious, hearing the cry, remembering how differently she had cried out in his arms that night.

The old man said something in a sharp voice. Nicolo ignored him. He went on kissing Aimee Black until her cry became a moan, until her mouth softened and clung to his.

Then he flung her from him, grabbed his briefcase and strode from the room.

Amazing, what an hour in a quiet place could do for a man's disposition.

An hour—and three bourbons, straight up.

Nicolo looked at the half inch of amber liquid that remained in his glass, sighed and pushed it away.

He was much calmer. Still furious at the Blacks and the ugly game he'd been dragged into, but at least he had regained his equilibrium.

What he needed now was coffee, perhaps a bite to eat. Then he'd go to his hotel, phone his pilot, have him ready the Learjet.

A few hours, and he'd be home.

Goodbye, New York. Goodbye, James Black. Goodbye, acquisition of Stafford-Coleridge-Black.

He could live without all of them. The city, the crazy old man, the bank.

There were other private banks in the United States, maybe not quite as suitable for his purposes, but they would do. He still had the short-list from which he'd ultimately chosen SCB. As soon as he returned to Rome, he'd tell his people to begin researching them in depth all over again.

It wasn't as if he'd fixated on this one financial institution....

As if he'd fixated on this one beautiful woman.

A lying, scheming, bitch of an immoral woman.

And, damn it, he didn't know why what had happened should have made him react with such rage.

The bartender caught his eye. Did he want another drink? Nicolo shook his head, then mouthed the word, *coffee*. The guy nodded.

He'd been around long enough to know that the days of the old robber barons were not over. Scandals in the world of high finance erupted as frequently as squalls over the Mediterranean. Seemingly intelligent men did amazingly stupid things to advance their own interests.

James Black was no different.

Neither was his granddaughter, who had been willing to sleep with a stranger to whet his appetite for a dynastic merger.

"Your coffee, sir."

Nicolo looked up. *"Grazie."*

"Will there be anything else?"

"Si." What was with all this Italian? When in Rome… or, in this case, New York… "Yes," he said. "A sandwich."

"What kind would you like?"

"Anything. Roast beef is fine." He smiled. "Something to keep the bourbon company, *si?*"

More Italian, he thought as the bartender moved off. A clear sign he was still distressed, though surely not anywhere near as much as before. The whiskey, now some much-needed logic, were working their magic.

The simple fact was that Black was a man who would do whatever was necessary to get what he wanted.

So would his granddaughter.

Nicolo drank some coffee.

And, really, how different did that make her from some other women he'd known? Women who dressed in a way meant to gain a man's interest. Who went to bed with a man and performed whatever tricks they imagined might win them points. Who lied to a man's face, promised love and devotion forever, all in hopes of landing a suitable husband.

Of all the women he'd known, Aimee Black was the last woman in the world he would ever consider marrying. Her morals were lacking and it wasn't because she'd slept with him that night.

It was because she'd done it as part of an act.

Nicolo took another mouthful of coffee.

Maybe his ego demanded it. Maybe his male pride required it. Whatever the reason, he'd wanted to believe that the woman with the violet eyes had felt the same un-controllable hunger he had felt. That she could no more have kept from making love with him than she could have stopped breathing.

That what had happened that night was the most ex-citing memory of her life, and that they had created that memory with equal passion and desire.

He could see her now, that night in his bed. Eyes dark with pleasure. Skin fragrant with her need...

"Your sandwich, sir."

Nicolo blinked. Had he ordered a sandwich?

"Would you like anything else? More coffee?"

Nicolo pushed the plate aside, rose to his feet and dropped a hundred-dollar bill on the table.

"No," he said brusquely, and added what he hoped was a polite smile and a hurried, *"Grazie."*

It wasn't the bartender's fault that what he wanted, what he damned well would not be denied, could not be found in this bar.

Aimee sat slumped on the sofa in her apartment, face buried in her hands.

Her anger was gone, replaced by a terrible emptiness in her heart.

"Let me explain," Grandfather had said.

Explain what? That he'd been willing to sell her to a foreigner to get what he wanted for his precious bank?

She'd fled his office, ignored his voice calling after her, stumbled into a taxi and gone home.

She'd never harbored any illusions about her grand-father's feelings for her. His lack of feelings, she amended, with a bitter smile. She'd accepted it.

What other choice did she have?

He'd taken her in after she'd lost her parents. He'd

raised her, or maybe it was more accurate to say he'd paid a series of nannies and housekeepers to raise her. He'd sent her to the best schools; he'd seen to it she had tennis and skiing and riding lessons, all the things his fortune could buy.

But he'd never really loved her.

What he loved was his bank and the dead Staffords, Coleridges and Blacks who'd founded it. Everything else, including her, was secondary.

Even so, she'd never dreamed him capable of such a cold-blooded scheme. That he'd want to marry her off to a stranger....

Except, Nicolo Barbieri—Prince Barbieri—was not a stranger. He was the man she'd made love with endless times in a few short hours.

How could she have done that? Climaxed in his arms when she hadn't even known his name?

Nausea roiled in her belly. Aimee clamped her hand to her mouth, raced to the bathroom and reached it just in time. A couple of moments later, pale and shaken, she flushed the commode and sank down on the closed seat.

God, she felt awful. She was tired of throwing up, tired of just plain feeling tired.

This time, at least she had a reason for feeling so rotten. Who wouldn't, after today?

That son of a bitch. Prince Barbieri. Prince of Darkness, was more like it. To call her a—a—

She couldn't even think the word.

How could he believe she'd deliberately seduced him? Offered herself as bait for her grandfather's vile proposition?

She'd slept with Nicolo Barbieri because—because she'd been upset. Anxious. Stressed.

Aimee groaned and put her face in her hands again.

She'd slept with him because she'd wanted to. Because he was the most exciting man she'd ever seen and because she'd fantasized about him all that afternoon.

That was why she'd refused to exchange names.

To make what had happened real would have meant despising herself for what she'd let him do....

And ever since that night, she'd wanted him to do it all again.

No wonder he'd looked at her with such loathing today. She loathed herself. But to believe she'd deliberately—

The ringing of the phone made her jump.

She didn't want to talk to anybody. Especially her grandfather and that was probably him calling. He was furious at her. She'd walked out of his office without a word, ignored his demand that she come back.

Let the answering machine deal with him. She wasn't going to.

Another ring. Then the machine picked up.

Hi. You've reached 555-6145. Please leave a message after the tone.

"Ms. Black, this is Dr. Glassman's office. Your test results are in. Please call our office between the hours of eight and—"

She ran for the phone, snatched it up. "I'm here! I mean, this is Ms. Black."

"Ms. Black? Please hold for the doctor."

Aimee held, imagining the worst. Why not, on a day like this? A brain tumor. A rare blood malady. Or—her breath caught at how stupid she was not to have thought of it sooner.

Or an illness of the kind people got these days, from having unprotected sex.

No. Not that.

Whatever else he was, she could not imagine the Prince of Darkness having that kind of disease.

"Ms. Black? Dr. Glassman here…"

Aimee listened. And listened. Then she put down the phone and stared blankly at the wall.

She'd thought right.

Nicolo Barbieri hadn't give her a disease.

He'd given her a baby.

She sat motionless for hours, wrapped in her robe, oblivious to the passage of time.

What to do? What to do?

She was single. Unemployed. Living on temporary jobs because she refused to let her grandfather support her.

No money, no prospects, this small apartment in a not-very-good neighborhood….

This time, it wasn't the phone that beat shrilly against the silence, it was the doorbell.

Aimee ignored it. Whoever it was would go away. The UPS man with a package, the super to drill a peephole in the door, something she'd been requesting for months.

The bell rang again. And again. Whoever was out there was persistent.

Aimee sighed, rose to her feet and went to the door. She undid the locks. The chain. Cracked the door an inch….

And felt the blood drain from her head.

"No," she said. "No—"

"Yes," Nicolo growled, and just as he had that fateful night, he put his shoulder to the door and forced it open.

CHAPTER SIX

THEY SAID TIME defused anger.

The hell it did.

In the thirty or forty minutes Nicolo had spent looking up Aimee Black in the telephone directory, then taking a taxi all the way downtown, through the tangled snarl of midmorning traffic, his anger didn't cool one bit.

If anything, it changed to something so hot and fierce he could damned near feel it inside him.

It was bad enough she'd been part of the ugly scam her grandfather had designed. If the actual seduction wasn't part of it, at least the come-on was.

What was worse was that she'd kept lying to him, not only that night but again this morning.

She had intended to entice him. He was certain of that. Now, she'd lied about what she'd felt in his arms. She hadn't intended to get caught up in her own game, but she had.

He was certain of it.

He knew women. The little things they did when they wanted to boost a man's ego. The things they did when their passion was real.

What Aimee felt had been real.

The throaty little moans. The soft cries. The lift of her

hips to his. Real. All of it. So real, he knew he'd never forget anything they had done together.

And he was damned well going to force her to admit it. She might have come on to him deliberately but after the first few minutes in his arms, everything had changed.

Aimee had followed where he led, all the way to ecstasy.

Dio, just thinking about it was making him hard, and if that wasn't ridiculous, he didn't know what was. He was a man who had his pick of women and even the occasional ones who started by pretending his touch drove them crazy soon forgot to pretend.

There were half a dozen women waiting for his return to Rome. One phone call, he'd have whichever of them he wanted ready to welcome him into her bed.

But he would be less a man if he didn't end this in a way that made it clear who was the victor, not just by walking out on the deal James Black had engineered but by forcing the old man's accomplice-in-crime to admit that what she'd felt in his arms had been real.

It was the penalty she'd pay for her duplicity.

Nobody lied to Nicolo Barbieri and got away with it, especially not a woman who had haunted his days and nights for three entire months.

The cab pulled up in front of a tired-looking, five-story tenement. James Black's granddaughter, Saturday night's party girl, lived here?

Maybe he had the address wrong.

There was only one way to find out.

Nicolo handed the cabbie a bill and told him to wait. Then he climbed the grimy steps to the front door. An unlocked front door.

Not a good idea in a neighborhood like this, but how Aimee lived was not his problem.

The door opened on a small vestibule, thick with the

faint but unmistakable odor of beer and other, less palatable things. The only signs of life were the mailboxes set into a stained gray wall.

Nicolo scanned the nameplates. A. Black lived in apartment 5C.

The door that opened into the house itself had no lock, either. None that was usable, anyway. Ahead, a dimly lit staircase with time-worn treads rose into the gloom.

Nicolo started up.

By the time he reached the fifth floor and apartment 5C, he was almost hoping he'd come to the wrong place. This was the kind of building that epitomized the things people tried to avoid when they lived in Manhattan.

So what? he told himself again. How Black's granddaughter lived was her affair.

He hesitated. Had coming here actually been a good idea? What would he gain by forcing her to admit she'd enjoyed what they'd done together? Was his ego that fragile, that it needed affirmation from a woman like this?

Before he could change his mind, Nicolo pressed the bell button.

Nobody answered.

He rang again. And then again. Okay. He'd come here, she wasn't home. That is, she wasn't home if he even had the correct address, which he doubted...

The door swung open. Not far, just a couple of inches, but enough for him to see the woman who'd opened it.

Aimee.

She stared at him. Her eyes widened. "No," she whispered, "no..."

What would come next was in those wide eyes. Besides, they had done this dance before.

She started to slam the door but Nicolo was too quick. She cried out and fell back as he put his shoulder to the door and forced it open. A second later, he was inside a tiny foyer.

Aimee was pressed against the wall, looking up at him with fear in her eyes.

He felt a tightening in his gut.

She hadn't been afraid of him that night… But this wasn't that night. It was good that she was afraid. Hell, it was what he wanted. When he was done with her…

"No," she said again, her voice high and thin.

Her eyes rolled up. She collapsed as if she were a marionette and someone had cut her strings.

Nicolo caught her before she crumpled to the floor. It was an automatic move but he knew damned well the faint was simply another outstanding performance….

Merda. His heart skipped a beat. It was not an act. She was limp in his arms.

He looked around frantically, saw a small sofa and carried her to it. "Ms. Black. Aimee. Can you hear me?"

Stupido! Of course she couldn't hear him. She was unconscious. What did you do for an unconscious woman?

Cold compresses. And spirits of—of what? Ammonia? Who in hell had spirits of ammonia lying around in this day and age?

A doorway opened onto a kitchen. Nicolo hurried inside, grabbed a towel from the sink, stuffed it with ice cubes from the fridge's freezer tray and ran back into the living room.

Aimee lay as he'd left her, small and unmoving, her pulse beat visible in her slender throat.

"Aimee," he said softly.

She didn't respond. Nicolo knelt beside her. Slipped his arm around her shoulders and lifted her to him.

"Aimee," he said again, and gently placed the ice pack against her forehead.

After a moment, she groaned.

"That's it, *cara*. Come on. Look at me. Open your eyes and look at me."

Her lashes fluttered but her lids stayed down. Nicolo drew her closer. Held her against him, eased her silky curls from the back of her neck and ran the ice pack lightly over the nape.

She moaned softly, her breath warm against his throat.

He closed his eyes.

He had forgotten what it was like to hold her. The delicacy of her bones. The floral scent of her hair. The unblemished softness of her skin.

His arms tightened around her. "Aimee," he whispered.

Suddenly he held a wildcat in his arms. She pulled back, curled her hands into fists and pounded them against his shoulders.

"Get away from me!"

"Aimee! Stop it!"

"What are you doing here?" Her voice shook. "Get out. Do you hear me? Get out!"

Nicolo grabbed her wrists in one hand. "Damn it, you fainted! Would you rather I'd left you lying on the floor?"

"I'd rather never see your face again!"

His mouth thinned. He let go of her and rose to his feet.

"My sentiments, exactly, Ms. Black. Where is your telephone?"

"What do you want with the telephone?"

"I'm going to phone for an ambulance. Then it will be my pleasure to walk out that door and not look back."

"No!" Aimee sat up quickly. Too quickly; the room seemed to give a sickening lurch and the all-too-familiar nausea sent a rush of bile up her throat. "I don't—I don't need an—"

"*Dio*, look at you! You're white as a ghost."

"I am fine," she said carefully, as she rose to her feet.

The room tilted again. She took a deep breath, then slowly let it out. "Thank you for your help, Prince Barbieri. Now, get the hell out of my apartment."

"Not until I know you're all right."

"Why would you give a damn?"

"Why? Well, let's see. I rang the bell. You opened the door, saw me and did an excellent imitation of a Victorian swoon." His smile was lupine and all teeth. "I'm sure you'll forgive me if I tell you I can envision a scenario in which you end up accusing me of somehow causing that swoon."

He meant it as an insult, she knew, but Aimee could only think how close to the truth he'd come.

"I just thanked you for your help, didn't I?"

"You're a superb liar," Nicolo said coldly. "Or did you think I'd forget that?"

"We've been all through this."

"Yes. We have. And you lied." His eyes narrowed as they met hers. "You told your grandfather I seduced you when we both know that what happened in that club, and in my hotel room, was by mutual consent."

Aimee stared up at him. His face might have been the stone face of a Roman emperor, his eyes unseeing and unfeeling. It was impossible to imagine she'd slept with this man.

He was, indeed, a stranger.

"Is that why you came here? To hear me admit that I—that I let you seduce me?"

"That you let me seduce you?" Nicolo folded his arms and gave a hollow laugh. "Such clever phrasing."

Aimee's legs were like rubber. She'd never fainted before but she thought she might damned well do it again if she had to keep up a conversation with this arrogant ass who was in a snit because he believed she'd come on to him deliberately.

She could only imagine how he'd react if he knew she carried a baby.

His baby.

A choked laugh caught in her throat. Prince Nicolo Barbieri's child. He wouldn't believe it. Well, who could blame him? She could hardly believe it, either.

She couldn't be pregnant. She took the pill. She'd been taking it for a couple of years now, not to prevent getting pregnant. Why would she, considering that the last time she'd been intimate with a man before she'd slept with Nicolo Barbieri was her senior year at college?

She took it to regulate her period, but what had happened to its primary function as a contraceptive?

Accidents happen. She could almost hear the tut-tutting voice of her boarding school's sex-ed teacher. *Remember, ladies, accidents happen.*

Her legs buckled.

"Dio!" Nicolo grabbed her shoulders as she collapsed on the sofa. "That's it. You need a doctor."

"I need you to go away." Aimee struggled up against the pillows as he took his cell phone from his pocket. "What are you doing?"

"Calling for an ambulance."

"No! I don't want an ambulance. Damn you, will you just—"

"Then tell me your physician's number."

Her physician's number. The man who'd made her pregnant wanted to call the doctor who'd just told her about that pregnancy. Wild laughter rose in her throat.

"You find this amusing?"

"No. Not amusing. Just—just…"

Aimee shook her head. The only thing she wanted was to bury her face in her hands and weep. That meant getting Nicolo Barbieri out of her apartment and out of her life.

Time to ditch her stupid pride.

"You came here to hear me admit that—that what happened between us was as much my idea as yours." She paused, touched the tip of her tongue to her dry lips. "All right. I admit it. I'm equally responsible for what happened." She shuddered and drew the lapels of her robe together. "I behaved irresponsibly. But not like—like what you called me. There was no plan. No orchestration. There was just—there was just you, and me, and some kind of insanity...."

Her voice faded away but she had said enough. Nicolo had what he'd come for: her admission that she'd wanted him as much as he'd wanted her.

The rest didn't matter. He knew that now.

He no longer gave a damn whose idea the meeting had been, hers or the old man. What mattered was that once he'd kissed her, once he'd touched her, she had belonged to him.

"Please. Go away now. I—I'm tired. I want to lie down."

His brow furrowed. She was more than tired. She looked... What? Ill? Frightened?

Terrified.

Of him? That was what he'd wanted, wasn't it? That she be afraid of him? And yet—and yet, suddenly, he wanted something more. Something just out of reach....

"Aimee." Nicolo squatted beside her and took her hands in his. Her fingers were ice-cold. "*Cara.* You need a doctor."

"No." She shook her head; the lustrous honey curls shifted like strands of heavy silk around her pale face. "I don't. Really. I'm fine."

Plainly, something was wrong. She needed help. He wanted to grab her and shake some sense into her.

Or take her in his arms and kiss her. Tell her she had

nothing to fear, not from him. Not from anything, as long as he was here to protect her....

Dio, was he losing his mind?

Nicolo shot to his feet. "Tea," he said briskly.

She looked up at him as if he'd lost his sanity. Perhaps he had but she wouldn't let him call a doctor and he'd be damned if he'd leave her when she looked like a ghost.

"Tea cures everything, or so my great-grandmother used to say."

Aimee didn't know whether to laugh or cry. He was human after all. He had to be, if he'd had a great-grand-mother.

She stood up. He reached out a steadying hand but she ignored it.

"Thank you for the suggestion," she said politely. "I'll make myself a cup of tea as soon as you— What?"

"I will make the tea."

He would make the tea. Aimee bit back another wave of what she knew was hysterical laughter.

This arrogant prince, this stranger who'd fathered the collection of cells in her womb, would make the tea.

That's all they were, at this point, weren't they? Just cells?

"You will drink some tea, and then I will leave." He smiled. "Agreed?"

His mood had changed. He'd gone from threatening to charming, and she knew the reason. It was because he'd gotten his way. He'd wrung a humiliating admission from her.

Oh, but his smile was devastating.

Maybe the realization showed in her face, because he moved closer and looked at her through eyes gone as dark as the sea.

"Aimee." His hands framed her face. "I'm sorry if I frightened you."

"You don't have to explain."

He shook his head, lay a finger lightly over her mouth.

"I was angry. At you. At your grandfather." He took a breath. "At myself, for wanting you so badly that night."

"Please—"

"I never wanted a woman as I wanted you." His voice roughened. "I think I might have died if you had turned me away."

What did a woman say to such an admission? That she'd have died, too, if he hadn't made love to her? That he'd made her feel things she'd never imagined? That she'd never forget that night in his arms?

All true—and now she carried his baby. For one moment, she'd forgotten that.

Aimee took a quick step back.

"The kettle's on the stove. The tea's in the cupboard over the sink. I'll—I'll just—I'll just go and wash my face…."

"Damn it, we have to talk about that night! You can't keep pretending it didn't happen."

Aimee shook her head, turned and fled. Just as she had that night, Nicolo thought, and thought, too, of what had happened when he caught her.

It would be the same now. All he had to was go after her….

"Damn it!"

He swung away, marched into the kitchen and grabbed the kettle. She had fainted. She was ill. What kind of animal was he to think of sex now?

Besides, he wasn't interested in getting involved with Aimee Black. As beautiful as she was, as much as he might want to make love to her, he'd never fully trust her

No matter what she claimed, he would always see James Black's hand in all that had—

The telephone rang.

Nicolo glanced toward the bathroom. The door was still closed; he could hear the sound of water running.

The phone rang again. Should he take the call? No. Surely she had voice mail….

Click.

Hi. You've reached 555-6145. Please leave a message after the tone.

A short metallic ring. Then a voice.

Hi, Ms. Black, this is Sarah from Dr. Glassman's office.

Nicolo put down the kettle. He knew he shouldn't listen to a private message but what was he supposed to do? Put his hands over his ears? Besides, this was from a physician.

Now, perhaps, he'd know why Aimee had fainted.

…vitamins. And iron. I meant to tell you that when we spoke earlier. Also, the doctor thought you might want a recommendation for an OB-GYN…

An OB-GYN? What in hell was that?

…absolutely fine, but it's always a good idea to start with an obstetrician early in your pregnancy and, of course, you're already in your third month….

The floor tilted under Nicolo's feet. *Pregnant?* Three months pregnant? What did it mean? What in hell did it mean that a woman he'd had sex with three months ago was—

Aimee flew past him and slapped the machine to silence. Her face had gone from white to red.

"Get out," she said. Her voice trembled as she pointed her finger at the door. "Damn it, Barbieri, do you hear me? Get out! Get out! Get—"

And with cold, relentless clarity, Nicolo knew. He knew exactly what it meant.

He had put a child in Aimee Black's belly.

CHAPTER SEVEN

AIMEE TRIED to tell herself this was all a bad dream.

Any second, she'd wake up, safe and in bed.

No phone messages from a receptionist who didn't understand the meaning of privacy. No Nicolo Barbieri staring at her like a man who'd just seen his life flash before his eyes.

Most of all, God, most of all, no baby growing inside her belly.

But it wasn't a dream.

Everything that was happening was hideously real, from the red light blinking with impersonal determination on her answering machine to the man standing in her tiny kitchen, dwarfing it with his size.

With his fury.

As if he had anything to be furious about.

It was she who was pregnant, she who would agonize over the life-changing decisions ahead, she who would pay the price for one night's madness.

Male and female. Yin and yang. Poets made the balance sound romantic but it wasn't. Men led. Women followed. That was what the world expected, and what too many women accepted.

She'd always known that. She'd watched her father treat

her mother like an amusing, if sometimes trying, possession.

Her grandfather had done his best to deal with her the same way but she hadn't permitted it. She'd *never* permitted it....

Until the night she fell into the arms of this stranger who stood watching her through accusing eyes.

At least she had herself under better control now. She took a steadying breath—there was no point in letting him see how upset she was—and looked straight back at him.

"Goodbye, Prince Barbieri."

It was like speaking to a statue. "Explain yourself," he growled.

Explain herself? The cold demand chased away whatever remained of her nerves.

She didn't need to explain herself to anyone.

"It's a small apartment," she said evenly. "Do you really need me to explain how to get to the front door?"

Her attempt at sarcasm backfired. The look on his face grew even colder.

"That call."

"That *private* call, you mean."

That, too, got her nowhere. "You are pregnant," he said flatly.

Aimee said nothing. Nicolo took a step toward her.

"Answer me!"

"You didn't ask a question."

His eyes narrowed. "I warn you, this is not a time for games." He jerked his head toward the telephone. "That message. Does it mean you are with child?"

Such an old-fashioned phrase. Another time, she might have found it charming. Now, she found it a measure of how much Nicolo Barbieri belonged in a world that was as far from her own as Earth was from the moon.

"That message was for me. I have no intention of discussing it with—"

He was on her before she could finish the sentence, his hands hard on her elbows as he lifted her to her toes.

"You are three months pregnant!" His grasp on her tightened. "Three months ago, you slept with me."

"I told you, I am not going to discuss this!"

"You will discuss whatever I wish, when it concerns me." He lowered his head until his eyes were on the same level as hers. "How many other men were you with three months ago?"

Oh, how she hated him! And yet, he had every right to think that way about her. She'd gone into his bed with no more planning than the slut he'd called her. With less planning, she thought, or she wouldn't be pregnant!

"I asked you a question."

"And I told you to get out." Aimee's voice trembled; she hated herself for the show of weakness. "You have no right—"

"You will answer me! How many others were there?"

She wrenched free of his hands. "A hundred. A thousand. Ten thousand! Are you satisfied?!"

The expression on his face was terrifying. She didn't care. Let him think whatever he liked. Let him think anything, so long as he went away and left her alone.

"I assume," he said, his voice clipped, "that is an exaggeration. Still, all things considered, do you actually know who the father is?"

She'd asked for the insult by her behavior that night and by her answer a moment ago. Still, it took all her control not to launch herself at him and claw out his eyes.

"Whoever it is, it isn't your problem."

"That is not an answer."

"It's the only one you're going to—"

He caught her again, pulled her roughly into his arms and kissed her savagely.

"Does that shake your memory, Aimee? Does it remind you that I have every right to demand answers—or have you forgotten I spent half the night spending myself inside you three months ago?"

Her face flamed. "I hate you," she said, struggling against his iron grip. "You're a bully. You're disgusting. You're—"

He kissed her again, harder than before, his lips, his teeth, his hands all a harsh reminder of his power.

"I am all that and more. Now answer the question. Who fathered the child you carry? Was it me?"

Her mind raced. All she had to do was say no. That would be the end of it.

And yet, how could she?

She didn't care about lying to Nicolo. But lying to the tiny life within her…

There was something terrible in that.

She knew thinking that way was crazy but everything that had happened today was crazy. Why not this, too?

Besides, the truth wouldn't change anything. This was her responsibility. She wasn't naïve; she knew how these things went. In school and then here in the city, she'd known women who'd been in the same fix. Things always ended the same way. The men denied being responsible. Or, if confronted by irrefutable proof, made some kind of settlement to avoid a nasty legal action and then went on with their lives.

The women ended up making decisions that would affect them forever. Abortion. Adoption. Single-mother-hood. Choose the one you hoped would be best for you, for your baby, then live with it.

This would be no different. Considering that Nicolo

hadn't already run out the door, his solution to the problem was surely going to be money.

Not that she gave a damn.

She was not weak. She could handle this on her own, and to hell with Nicolo Barbieri.

The sooner he understood that, the better.

"Is this baby mine?" he demanded.

Aimee looked up in defiance. "You're goddamned right it is."

Except for the almost-painful tightening of his hands on her flesh, he showed no emotion.

"You are certain?"

An ugly question, but she didn't flinch. "Absolutely."

"There was no one else who could have—"

"No."

"Because, I promise you, Aimee, I will demand blood tests."

"What you'd want is a DNA test," she said coldly. "They're a much more reliable proof of paternity, according to a law class I took in college." She smiled thinly. "But bothering with the test would be a waste of time."

His lips drew back from his teeth in what might have been an attempt at a smile.

"That decision will be mine. It will not be yours."

His accent was growing more and more pronounced. She'd already figured out that was a sure sign he was having trouble controlling his temper.

Too bad.

She had a temper, too. And there was a limit to how many insults a woman, even an imprudent one, had to take.

"Believe me, Prince Barbieri. I've only done a few foolish things in my life." Aimee jerked free of his hands. "And going to bed with you rates as number one."

His face darkened. "Insulting me at a time like this is not wise."

"Then don't insult me by calling me a liar! You asked the question. I answered it. Unfortunately you don't like the answer, but that doesn't change that fact that it was you who made me pregnant."

"I *made* you pregnant." His words were filled with soft malice. "Such an interesting way to phrase what happened that night, *cara*."

She felt the heat rise in her cheeks. "What happened was that I'd had too much to drink."

"I don't recall you having anything to drink."

His assessment was closer to the mark than hers. She'd had one drink. Actually, a couple of sips of one drink, but she wasn't going to be sidetracked into a discussion of why she'd had sex with him when she didn't understand it herself.

"The point is, you impregnated me."

"Now you describe a laboratory experiment." He moved toward her slowly, gaze locked to hers, and though she hated herself for it, she took a step back. "But that was not what happened in that bathroom or in my bed."

"There is no reason to have this conversation."

"Ah, but there is." He was a breath away now, his eyes glittering with heat as her shoulders hit the wall. "I think you need reminding of what we did that night."

"I have all the reminding I need."

"*Si.* So it would seem. My child in your womb." His gaze flattened. "Was this part of the great plan?"

Aimee blinked. "What?"

"Such an innocent face, *cara*." His mouth twisted with derision. "And such a devious scheme. The clever meeting on the street. The coincidental meeting at the club. The seduction." He cupped her face, raised it to his until the midnight-blue of his eyes filled her vision. "And now, this. An heir to your grandfather's kingdom. A child of my blood from the womb of a Stafford-Coleridge-Black descendant." His gaze darkened. "Such an amazing set of coincidences."

"You are," Aimee whispered shakily, "an evil man."

"I am a logical man. One who assumed you were using protection."

"I was. It failed."

"How convenient it failed when failure was most necessary."

Her eyes filled with angry tears. "I despise you!"

"That really breaks my heart, *cara*."

"When I think that—that I let you touch me—"

"You *let* me touch you?" Nicolo gave a sharp bark of laughter. "You begged me to touch you. I remember every word. Every whisper."

"I must have been out of my mind."

Aimee's face was white with exhaustion. Clearly this was taking its toll and, just for a second, Nicolo's anger lessened.

She was pregnant. And she had been so ill just a short while ago….

So what? he thought coldly.

She had brought it all on herself. Did she really expect him to believe her birth control protection had failed? A woman like her… Surely she would know all about such things.

And what about you?

The thought whispered its way from the depths of his conscience. He had to admit, it was a fair question.

He had taken Aimee without a condom. And he always used a condom, even if a woman said it wasn't necessary. Perhaps he was old-fashioned but protection was a man's responsibility, especially in today's sometimes ugly world.

So, what had become of his sense of responsibility that night?

It had flown out the window along with the ability to think with his brain instead of his body.

He'd wanted Aimee more than he'd ever wanted a woman in his life. *Dio,* he was getting hard, just remembering.

Nicolo cursed, spun away from her and paced across her kitchen. He ran his hands through his hair and told himself he was crazy.

His entire world had been upended and he was thinking about what it had been like to make love to a woman who was a stranger to him in every way that mattered.

What he had to think about was not that. It was what he should do next.

Should he contact his attorney? Demand to speak with her physician? What were his financial responsibilities, now and in the future?

Whenever an acquaintance married and had a child, he'd think, yes, I suppose I shall have a son, too, sometime in the future. Perhaps because his father had hardly ever been around when he was growing up, being a parent had never seemed anything more than a vague idea.

Now, it was fast becoming reality, assuming a lab test said Aimee Black was telling the truth. Assuming she wanted to remain pregnant.

Nicolo's jaw tightened.

That would, of course, be her decision.

But it was a great deal to take in all at once. A child. His child. In the womb of a woman who had stirred him so that he'd forgotten everything he'd ever known about self-control.

To hell with that. Angry at Aimee, angry at himself, he swung toward her again.

"I assume you've made plans."

"They don't concern you."

"What are those plans?"

"I just said—"

"Whatever you do, you will need proper care."

"Didn't you hear me? What I do is not your concern."

"The message from your doctor. I gather he found you well."

"*She* found me well," Aimee said, with a lift of her chin.

Could a man laugh at such a moment? Nicolo found that at least he could smile.

"I stand corrected. And this—this OP?"

"OB-GYN. And we're not going to have this conversation."

"This is a specialist?"

"Damn it, Barbieri—"

"I see I am no longer that magnificent creature, the prince," he said dryly.

"You are an intruder. And I want you to out of my home immediately."

"What is this OB-GYN?"

"An obstetrician. Must I phone the police to get rid of you?"

"And tell them what, *cara?* That it annoys you to discuss your pregnancy with the man responsible for it?" He flashed a thin smile. "I suspect the officers who respond to your call would enjoy something to lighten their day."

"Nicolo." Her voice was weary. "Why are you doing this?"

He strode to her and cupped her elbows. "I am doing it," he said sharply, "because you claim my child lies in your belly."

"You asked for the truth. Don't blame me if..." Aimee gasped and tried to catch his hands. "What are you doing?"

"Opening your robe," he said calmly, as he undid the sash. "I want to see this pregnancy of yours."

"I told you, it's not..." Her breath caught as he spread the lapels of her robe wide. "Damn you, Nicolo—"

"It is my right," he said coldly.

It was. Wasn't it? The right of a man to see the body of a woman who claimed she carried his baby?

Dio, he had almost forgotten how beautiful she was.

The night they met, she'd worn something wickedly sexy under that incredible crimson dress. A black bra. A black thong. Both silky and small enough to hold in the palm of his hand.

Now, she wore sensible white cotton. A bra and panties. And it didn't matter. She had the kind of body that didn't need black silk to make it sexy.

Was it too soon to see the changes his child would bring? Her belly was still flat. Her breasts...were they already a little fuller?

"Nicolo." Her voice was husky. "Nicolo..."

"I'm just curious, *cara.*" His voice was husky, too. And rough. As rough as the sudden pounding of his heart. He reached out, placed his hand over her belly again. "Still flat," he said, as if it didn't matter that he could feel the heat of her skin through the plain white cotton panties.

"Nicolo."

He looked up, his eyes dark as they met hers. She was trembling; her lips were slightly parted and he remembered how they had parted for him that night. How greedily he had tasted her mouth. Her ineffable sweetness.

"What of your breasts?" he said in a low voice. Eyes locked to hers, he cupped one delicate mound of flesh. She gave a little moan; her eyes went from violet to black. "Have they changed yet?"

He felt her nipple engorge behind the cotton of her bra. She moaned again as he moved his thumb across the swollen tip and he knew he could have her. Take her again and again, until he'd rid himself of this need to possess her….

Dio, perhaps he *had* lost his mind! Quickly he stepped back.

"So," he said briskly, as if nothing had happened, "we must discuss what to do next. What is right."

Aimee pulled her robe together. She was shaken; he could see it, but he could see that she wasn't going to admit it.

"What is right," she said, "is for you to get out of my life."

"I intend to as soon as we settle this."

"It's settled. This is my problem and I'll decide what's right."

Nicolo nodded, but was that correct? Was the choice solely hers? What did a man do at a time like this? He'd never had to make the decision but he knew the obvious answers.

The trouble was that the obvious answers didn't apply when you were the man involved in actually making the decision.

And what a hell of a decision this was.

He had made Aimee Black pregnant. Forget the nonsense about other men. He had always trusted his gut instinct in business; he trusted it now. He would own up to his responsibility, financially.

That was his decision.

What she did after that was hers.

Nicolo reached into his pocket, took out his checkbook and a gold pen.

"I don't want your money!"

He looked up. Aimee was watching him, her eyes almost feverish in her pale face.

"You said you will do whatever is right. And so shall I." He uncapped the pen. "Five hundred thousand. Will that be—"

"Five hundred thousand dollars?"

His eyebrows rose. "Is it not enough?"

Aimee flew at him and slapped the checkbook and pen from his hand. "Get out," she growled. "Get out, get out, get—"

"Damn it," Nicolo snarled, grabbing her wrists before she could slug him, "are you insane?"

"Do you think your money can change what's happened? That it can buy back my dignity?" Tears of anger rose in her eyes to glitter like jewels on her lashes. "I don't want your money, Nicolo. I don't want anything from you except your promise that I'll never see your face again!"

Her tears fell on his hand like the rain that had fallen on them both the day they'd met.

He suspected he would never forget that meeting, or Aimee.

Her defiance. Her passion. Her determination.

An inadvertent smile lifted the corner of his mouth. If ever a man wanted sons—even daughters—Aimee would be the woman to bear them. Such fire. Such courage...

His breath caught.

Suddenly he knew what was right. How had it taken him this long to see it?

He let go of Aimee's hands. Then he picked up his checkbook, retrieved his pen, put them both back in his pocket. A roll of paper towels hung over the kitchen sink. He tore off half a dozen sheets and held them out to her.

She shoved them away.

"I just said, I don't want anything from you!"

"Perhaps you'll make an exception," he said calmly, "considering that your nose is running."

She flushed, grabbed the towels, put them to her nose and gave a long, noisy blow.

"Much better."

"Good. I wouldn't want to offend Your Highness's delicate sensibilities."

Her voice was shaky but he could see her self-control returning. He had the feeling she was going to need it.

"I know you're being sarcastic, *cara*, but—"

"Such perception!"

"—but, sarcasm aside, it's inappropriate to address me by my title."

Aimee burst out laughing. "Now you're going to give me lessons in court etiquette? God almighty, what a horrible human being you—"

"I do not believe in such formality," he said, cursing himself for a fool because he knew damned well a man couldn't sound more formal than he did right now. He paused, took a breath and got on with it. "Particularly from the woman who is about to become my wife."

CHAPTER EIGHT

MARRY HIM?

Marry Nicolo Barbieri.

The man who had seduced her. And he had, no matter what he claimed. He'd started it all. Followed her into that bathroom. Locked the door. Lifted her onto the marble vanity. Torn aside her panties.

Thrust deep into her…and even now, despite everything, just thinking of what it had been like made her body quicken.

What was the matter with her, that she should still feel desire for him? She couldn't blame him for making her pregnant—she hadn't been thinking any more clearly than he that night—but there was no escaping that he'd made love to her….

And then called her a slut because he believed she'd been part of some ugly scheme of her grandfather's.

Why wouldn't he think that? Nicolo was every bit as ruthless and driven as the coldhearted old man who'd raised her.

James was willing to sell her for the good of his kingdom. Nicolo was willing to buy her for the same reason. He'd probably been willing to do it from the instant her grandfather suggested it.

All that indignation this morning, the fiery show of contempt for her and her grandfather, had been a lie to placate his own ego. He'd needed to justify a devil's bargain and she and her answering machine had handed it to him, all prettily gift-wrapped and tied with a great big bow.

She was pregnant with his baby. What better way to agree to marrying her than by making it seem a gallant gesture?

Except, she knew the truth.

The Prince of All He Surveyed was about as gallant as a fifteen-century monarch weighing the benefits of a royal marriage—except for one enormous difference.

No matter what he thought, she wasn't governed by the rules of James Black's kingdom. She was not a princess. She didn't have to marry a tyrant she didn't know, didn't love, didn't even like.

"Well, *cara?* Has my proposal swept you off your feet, or shall I take your silence as wholehearted agreement?"

Aimee looked up. Nicolo's words were sarcastic but his eyes were cool and watchful. He had to know she wasn't going to agree—or maybe he didn't. He was just arrogant enough, imperious enough, to assume his proposal—and wasn't that an amazing thing to call it—was everything a woman in her situation could want.

She almost laughed. He was in for one hell of a surprise!

Learning she was pregnant, having to make all the tough choices that came next without anyone to help her, was the most terrifying thing that had ever happened.

Only one thing could possibly be more frightening: marriage to a man like the Evil Prince.

Aimee tossed her head, as if none of this was worth discussion.

"I have lots to say," she said evenly. "But for both our

sakes, I'll stay with thanks but no thanks and, oh, by the way, don't let the door hit you in the butt on your way out."

Good, she thought. Not original, but concise. She'd have liked it better if he showed some reaction but he didn't. No look of surprise. Not even anger. All he did was smile and, God, she hated that smile, the all-knowing insolence of it.

"Perhaps 'proposal' is the wrong word," he said smoothly.

"At least we can agree on that. 'Decree' is the word that came to my mind." Aimee smiled, too, and lifted her chin. "There's only one problem. You may be a prince but I'm not one of your subjects. Your ridiculous pronouncements don't mean a thing to me."

"So much for my attempt at being gallant."

She'd been right. And what was that tiny twinge of regret all about? She knew she was a pawn in a game played between Nicolo and her grandfather.

Now, *he* knew that she knew it.

Dark Knight takes pawn. Checkmate.

"That's unfortunate, Aimee." Another of those quick, infuriating smiles lifted one corner of his mouth. "The easiest path to a goal is generally the preferable one."

"And the easiest path to the door is right behind you. Goodbye, Nicolo. I hope I never have the misfortune of seeing you again."

Still no reaction. Damn it, she wanted one! Didn't the man know when he was being insulted?

Apparently not.

Instead of heading for the door, he picked up the things he'd dropped and took a little black notebook from his pocket, flipped it open, found the page he wanted and frowned.

"Wednesday," he said briskly. His frown deepened.

"No. On second thought…" Another glance, a nod, and then he scrawled something with the pen. "I must be in Rome by Wednesday but I am free tomorrow." The pen and notebook went back into his pocket; he folded his arms and looked at her, his expression unreadable. "Will ten in the morning be suitable?"

"I have no idea what you're talking about."

"For our marriage, *cara*. What else have we been discussing?"

Aimee laughed. That, finally, got a reaction. Oh, if looks could kill…

"You find this amusing?"

"Actually I find it incredible. I'm sure people trip over their feet in an effort to please you but here's a news flash, Prince." Her laughter faded; her face became as stony as his. "I am not marrying you."

"You are pregnant."

"I am pregnant. *I* am pregnant," she repeated, pounding her fist between her breasts for emphasis. "And *I* am perfectly capable of handling the situation myself."

"What happened is my responsibility."

"A little while ago you were busy saying it was mine."

"I was wrong." He drew himself up. "I am the man and such things are a man's duty."

Another time, the ridiculous speech might have made her roll her eyes. Not now. He meant it. Or wanted to think he meant it. Or wanted *her* to think he meant it.

Anything, to get his hands on her grandfather's bank and extend the scope and power of the Barbieri empire.

"How nice," she said softly. "And how amazing, that you should turn into this—this ethical creature instead of the son of a bitch we both know you—"

A cry broke from her throat as he clasped her shoulders.

"Call me whatever you like. Hate me as much as

pleases you. It changes nothing. I live by a set of rules that necessitate I accept responsibility for my actions." His grasp on her eased. "Perhaps it took me a while to accept that but what I learned just now took me by surprise."

"Have you ever counted how many times you use the words 'I' and 'me' and 'my'? Try it sometime. You might be surprised. Oh, and here's another thing that might surprise you." She pulled free of his hands. "Did you think I wouldn't notice that marrying me will drop Stafford-Coleridge-Black right into your hands?"

"An undeniable fact, I agree."

"Then, let me be more direct." Aimee's eyes were hot with warning. "I will not marry you under any—"

Nicolo cursed, grabbed her, hauled her into his arms and captured her mouth with his. It was sudden; she had no time to think, no time to do anything except let it happen….

No time to keep her lips from parting hungrily under the pressure of his.

When he drew back, she stood motionless, heart racing, body tingling, while he watched her through narrowed eyes.

"There is an American expression," he said softly. "Win-win. Do you know it, *cara?* It is the perfect way to describe what I have in mind."

"I know what you have in mind. And I don't want any part of it."

"Your grandfather wants an heir. I want SCB."

"And you'd marry me to get it."

"James says you are an intelligent woman. Can't you see beyond your pride?"

Did he think that was why she wouldn't agree? Because of her pride? Did he think that if he'd wanted her—*her,* not an expansion of his empire—she'd have agreed to this outrageous marriage?

"You're right," she said, her voice shaking, "I do have too much pride to marry someone like you."

His eyes went cold. "This discussion is over."

"You said that before. And I agree. It's over. So are your pathetic attempts to convince me to marry you."

"I was going to tell you that I would be willing to let you try your hand at helping me run SCB, once it is mine." His mouth thinned. "Now, I would not even allow you to play at being in charge of the mail room."

"What a coldhearted bastard you are."

"No," he said calmly, "not at all. For all intents and purposes, I had no father. I would wish better for my child."

"Such a noble sentiment! Too bad I know that this is all about SCB. Well, I don't give a damn for SCB! And nothing you say or do can make me change my mind."

Nicolo smiled thinly. "I wonder if you'll feel that way when I tell your grandfather that you carry my child, that I have offered to marry you and that you have refused."

"Do it," she said recklessly. "I hate you. I hate him—"

"You may hate me, *cara*, but you don't hate that old man. If you did, you wouldn't have been so hurt by the things he said this morning." His gaze hardened. "Your grandfather hasn't much longer to live," he said bluntly. "Would you have him die knowing you denied him the things only you can give him?"

Aimee knotted her hands. "Is there anything you won't do to get your own way?"

"Win-win, *cara*," he said softly. "A peaceful close to your grandfather's long life. Legitimacy for our child." He drew her against him, his arousal swift and obvious against the V of her thighs. "And a bonus," he said, his voice low and rough. "Or must I remind you what it was like when we made love?"

"It was sex, not love. And if you really think I'd ever let you touch me again—"

Nicolo laughed, gathered her against him and kissed her.

She struggled. Fought. But his kiss was deep and all-consuming and in a heartbeat, she was kissing him back.

It was the same as the night they'd met.

The fire. The hunger. The heavy race of her heart. The only way she could keep from falling was to clutch his jacket, rise on her toes, cling to him and cling to him until he let go of her.

It took a moment to catch her breath. By then, he had strolled to the door.

"Ten o'clock," he said over his shoulder. "And be prompt. I don't have time to waste."

"You—you—"

Blindly she snatched a glass from the counter and flung it. It shattered against the wall an inch from his head but he didn't turn around. If he had—if he had, he thought grimly as he yanked the door open and went into the hall, God only knew what he'd have done.

There was a limit to how much of a woman's anger a man had to take.

Halfway down the stairs, he took out his cell phone and called his attorney.

"This is Nicolo Barbieri. I wish to be married tomorrow," he said brusquely, aware and not giving a damn that this was exactly the kind of arrogance Aimee had accused him of. "The woman's name is Aimee Stafford Coleridge Black." He listened for a moment, then made an impatient sound. "Rules and regulations are your concern, *signore,* not mine. Find a way around them, make the necessary arrangements and send a report, the paperwork, whatever is necessary, to me at my hotel. No, not as soon as you can. Tonight."

Nicolo snapped his phone shut and stepped into the street. It was raining again. *Dio,* what was with this combination? Rain, and Aimee Black. It was as if the skies were trying to tell him something. He had no coat, no umbrella and from what he could see, there wasn't a subway station in the vicinity. No bus stops, either, and as always when it rained in Manhattan, the taxis seemed to have vanished.

He was at least forty blocks from his hotel.

He began walking. The exercise would do him good. Maybe he could work off some of his anger.

Aimee wasn't the only one who was furious.

He was, too.

At her. At himself. At how easily she could make him lose his grip on logic and self-control, the very qualities that had helped him build what she so disparagingly referred to as his kingdom.

He knew men who lived on the largesse of those impressed by a useless title.

Not Nicolo.

He had worked hard for all he had, though Aimee made it clear she didn't think so. She didn't like him. Didn't respect him.

Why in hell was he going to marry her?

To gain Stafford-Coleridge-Black? Ridiculous. He wanted it, yes, but not enough to tie himself to a woman he didn't love.

To give her unborn child a name? He wasn't even sure the child was his. How had he forgotten that?

And even if it was, he didn't need to marry Aimee to accept the responsibilities of paternity. He could even make it a point to be part of the child's life.

Well, as much as he could.

If he'd been calmer, he'd have seen all this right away. But Aimee had forced a confrontation. Her anger had fueled his and he'd let her wrest control of the situation from him.

She was good at that.

The only time he'd been in command was the night he'd made love to her. She had been his. Moaning at his touch. Sighing at his kisses. Trembling under his caresses.

Nicolo cursed.

It had been nothing more than sex, as she'd so coldly pointed out. It was just that the passage of time had made it seem more exciting than it had actually been.

And even if it had been extraordinary, why would he want to tie himself to her? To any woman, but especially to this one, who had the disposition of a tigress?

That was fine in bed but out of it a man wanted a sweet-tempered, obedient woman. He knew dozens like that, every one beautiful and sexy and a thousand times easier to handle.

Which brought him back to reality and the knowledge that he couldn't come up with a single, rational reason to go through with this wedding, and what a hell of a relief that was.

Nicolo slowed his steps. The rain had stopped. The sun was out. Taxis prowled the streets again. He hailed one, got inside and told the driver the name of his hotel.

He would go to Aimee's apartment at ten tomorrow morning because he had said that was what he would do, but when he arrived, he'd tell her he'd changed his mind, that he didn't want to marry her.

He'd tell her the rest, too, that he would support the child—and her, of course—and, in general, do the right thing.

Problem solved.

Nicolo folded his arms, sat back and smiled. He was soaked to the skin but he was happy.

* * *

Hours later, the bellman delivered a thin manila envelope from Nicolo's attorney.

A note inside assured him that all he had to do in the morning was take the attached documents and his prospective bride to a building in lower Manhattan, ask for a particular judge and he and the lady in question would be married within the hour.

That there was no longer a prospective bride was beside the point. The papers were simply a reminder of how foolish he'd almost been, and he shoved them aside.

He went to bed at eleven. At midnight, he got up and paced the confines of the suite. When he lay down again more than an hour later, he fell into troubled sleep. His dreams were murky and unpleasant, involving a small boy wandering the somber halls of Stafford-Coleridge-Black in search of something nameless and elusive. Each time the child was on the verge of finding it, Nicolo woke up.

At dawn, he gave up, phoned down for coffee, rye toast and the *Times* and the *Wall Street Journal*. Showered, shaved and dressed in chinos and a navy shirt with the sleeves rolled up, he sat by the sitting room window to have his breakfast and read the papers.

The coffee was fine. The toast was dry. So was the writing in both the *Times* and the *Journal*. Why else would he be unable to focus on any of the articles?

Nicolo tossed them aside and checked his watch for what had to be the tenth time since he'd awakened. Seven-thirty. Too early to show up at Aimee's door and tell her she could forget about marrying him.

He could imagine how happy that would make her. She might even smile, something he hadn't seen her do since the night he'd taken her to bed.

He was happy, too. If he was feeling grim, it was only because he wanted to get the damned thing over with.

Seven forty-five.

Seven fifty.

Seven fifty-seven.

"Merda," Nicolo snarled, and shot from his chair.

He could arrive at Aimee's any time he wanted. There was no right time to deliver good news. Besides, she didn't have to be ready. She wasn't going anywhere.

Traffic was heavy and it was almost eight-thirty when he climbed the steps to Aimee's building. Yesterday's rain hadn't done much to clean the grungy stoop.

The first thing he'd do would be to buy her a condo in a decent neighborhood.

This was not a fit place to raise her child.

He paused outside her apartment, then rang the bell. He rang it again. She might be in the shower, getting ready for his arrival. Or, knowing Aimee, *not* getting ready.

It almost made him smile.

Whatever else she was, she was brave. He'd never known a woman to stand up to him before. He knew damned well yesterday's argument wasn't over. The second she opened the door and saw him, she'd lift her chin in that way she had and tell him what he could do with his marriage proposal.

He'd let her rant for a few seconds and then he'd say, *There is no proposal*, cara. *I have decided I would sooner live with a scorpion than with you.*

The door opened.

Everything he'd anticipated was wrong.

Aimee didn't lift her chin. She didn't rant. And, even though he'd shown up more than an hour early, he could see that she had been waiting for him.

She wore a simple yellow sundress and white sandals

with little heels. Her hair was pulled into a ponytail, her face was bare of makeup and her eyes were suspiciously bright as if she'd been crying.

She looked painfully young, heartbreakingly vulnerable—and incredibly beautiful.

For one wild moment, Nicolo imagined taking her in his arms, telling her she had nothing to be afraid of. That he would be good to her, that he would take care of her...

He frowned, then cleared his throat.

"Aimee. I have come to tell you—"

"What? More threats?" Her chin rose now, just as he'd expected. "Let me save you the trouble." She took a shaky breath. "I thought it through." She gave an unsteady laugh. "Actually, it's all I thought about since you left yesterday. And—and you're right, Nicolo. I have no choice but to marry you."

He stared at her in disbelief. *Say something,* he told himself, *tell her you've changed your mind!*

"You were right. About my grandfather. I want to hate him but I can't. He raised me. He gave me all the things he believed I needed and if I needed more, his love, his respect..."

Aimee stopped the rush of words. Why bare her soul? She was going to marry Nicolo Barbieri. That was enough.

"He's old," she continued, her voice low. "And growing frail. I don't want to look back after he's gone and know I denied him the only things he ever asked of me, the bank in your hands, and—" color rose in her cheeks "—and your child."

Nicolo said nothing. After a few seconds, Aimee cleared her throat. "So, I'll marry you."

"But?" His smile was thin. "Don't look so surprised, *cara*. One would have to be deaf not to have heard that unspoken word."

"This marriage—it will be in name only. A legal convenience that will end on my grandfather's death."

Aimee waited, trying to read Nicolo's expression, but it told her nothing.

"No sex," he finally said, his voice silken.

She nodded. "None."

"And tell me, *cara*. What am I to do when I want sex?"

The seemingly subservient woman of the last few moments disappeared. Aimee's eyes flashed with her old defiance.

"You'll do whatever you must but you'll be discreet about it."

Nicolo burst out laughing. She felt her hands ball. How she wanted to slap that laugh from his face!

"Let me be sure I understand this. I marry you. I give you my name. My title. And at some point in the future, we divorce and I end up with alimony payments and child support. In return for all this, you will not complain when I keep a mistress. Is that right?"

He didn't wait for an answer. Instead he swept her into his arms and drew her against him.

"Here is how it will be," he growled. "You will be my wife. You will be available to me whenever I wish. Night. Day. Anywhere, anytime. If I also want a mistress, I will have one."

"I won't marry you under those conditions!"

"*Si*. You will. And if there is a divorce, it will be because I have wearied of you." She tried to wrench free; his hold on her tightened. "And before you say, 'no, Nicolo, I won't marry you under those conditions,' consider this." He leaned toward her, eyes glittering. "I can take this child from you the day it's born. Do not shake your head! I am Prince Nicolo Antonius Barbieri. No court would deny me the right to my own flesh and blood. Is that clear?"

"You no good, evil, vicious bastard," she hissed, "you son of a—"

Nicolo captured her mouth with his, kissed her again and again until she trembled in his arms.

Then he picked up the small suitcase near her feet and jerked his head toward the door.

CHAPTER NINE

SOME WOMEN dreamed about their weddings.

Would the day be sunny? What kind of gown? Would it be sweet and romantic, like something Scarlett would have worn in *Gone with the Wind*, or would it be sexy and sophisticated? And then there was all the rest. The setting. The attendants. The guests. The flowers.

Aimee was glad she'd never wasted time on such silly dreams, otherwise—otherwise what was happening now might make her weep. A high-ceilinged room in a tired municipal building. A judge who'd seemed surprised to see them until his secretary whispered something in his ear. A pair of witnesses plucked from the clerical staff.

And Nicolo, her stern-faced groom, standing beside her.

Oh, yes. It was a damned good thing she'd been too busy studying to think about weddings.

Marriage had only been a distant possibility. Friends had married; Aimee had smiled and said all the right things but mostly she'd thought, *Not me, not yet, maybe not ever.*

She had things to do, a life to live, and if she ever did marry, it would be someone the exact opposite of her grandfather.

Yet today she was marrying a man who made her grandfather look like a saint, a stranger taking her as his wife as if they'd been sent back to a time when men and women married for reasons of—

"Miss?"

—for reasons of title and expediency that had nothing to do with love or romance or—

"Miss?"

Aimee blinked. The judge smiled in apology.

"Your name again, miss? I'm terribly sorry but—"

"No," Aimee replied, "that's all right, Your Honor. I understand."

She did. She understood it all. The impersonal setting, the equally impersonal words. Why would he remember her name?

The only surprise came when it was time for Nicolo to put a ring on her finger.

The cold stranger who'd made it clear this would be a marriage on his terms, who'd undoubtedly browbeaten some poor soul at City Hall into issuing a marriage license in less than twenty-four hours, had neglected to buy a wedding ring.

Admitting his error made him blush. It was lovely to see, she thought with dour satisfaction.

"I don't need a ring," she said coolly. Coolly enough so even the two bored witnesses looked at her.

"My wife needs a ring," Nicolo said grimly, tugging one she'd never before noticed from his finger. "We will use this," he said, his accent thick enough to trip over.

The ring was obviously old, its slightly raised crest almost worn away, and it was so big that Aimee had to clench her fist to keep it from falling off.

That was fine.

Clenching her fist helped keep her from screaming, "Stop!"

But there was no going back. In the dark hours of the

night, agreeing to this marriage had seemed the only thing she could do. For her grandfather and, yes, for her baby. Her unborn child was entitled to be free of the stain of illegitimacy.

The arrangement could work, she'd told herself as she sat by the window, staring blindly out at the neighboring brick tenement that was her entire view. Her child would get his father's name. Nicolo would get the bank. She would get the satisfaction of giving her grandfather the one thing not even his vast fortune could buy.

It would all be very civilized…and how could she have been stupid enough to believe that? If only she'd kept her mouth shut. Telling Nicolo she'd marry him but she wouldn't sleep with him had been like waving a bone at a caged and hungry wolf.

It only made him want what he couldn't have.

She shouldn't have said anything. After all, he couldn't force her to sleep with him. Nicolo Barbieri was a tyrant, but he wasn't a savage.

Was he?

God oh God, what was she doing?

What had she been thinking?

Aimee swung toward Nicolo, oblivious to the judge, the witnesses, the ceremony.

"Nicolo," she said urgently, "wait…"

"…husband and wife," the judge said, and offered an election-year smile. "Congratulations, Prince Barbieri. Oh, and Princess Barbieri, of course. Sir, you may kiss your bride."

Nicolo looked at her. His eyes told her he knew exactly what she'd been about to say; the proof came when he bent his head and put his mouth to her ear.

To the onlookers, it probably looked as if he was whispering something tender but it was hardly that.

"Too late, *cara*," he murmured, the words a steel fist in a velvet glove.

Then he shook the judge's hand, thanked the witnesses and drew Aimee's arm through his.

"Time for the newlyweds to be alone," he said, with a little smile.

The judge and the witnesses laughed politely.

Aimee trembled.

He'd told the taxi driver to wait by circling the block; the cab appeared just as they came down the courthouse steps.

Nicolo opened the door, motioned Aimee inside and climbed in next to her.

"Kennedy," he said. "The General Aviation facility."

Aimee stared at him as the cab pulled into midmorning traffic. "What?"

"The airport. The area where corporate jets are—"

"I know what Kennedy is," she said impatiently. "But why are we going there?"

Nicolo raised a dark eyebrow. "Where did you think we would go, *cara?*" His smile was silken. "Are you in such a rush to be alone with me that you hoped we'd go to my hotel?"

No way was she going to let him draw her into that kind of conversation! Aimee folded her hands in her lap.

"I asked you a question. Do you think you could give me a straight answer?"

His smile faded. "We're going home."

Home? She stared at him blankly. They hadn't discussed where they'd live but then, they hadn't discussed much of anything.

"Did you think we would live in New York?"

That was precisely what she'd thought.

"My home is in Italy," he said brusquely. "In Rome. My

house is there, my corporate headquarters… Don't look so stricken, *cara*. New York isn't the center of the world."

It was the center of *her* world. Didn't he see that?

"But—but—"

"If you're concerned about not packing enough clothes, you can shop tomorrow."

Did he think this was about clothes? She would have laughed, except laughter was too close to tears.

"I'm not concerned about that."

"If it's because we haven't told your grandfather, don't be. I'll call him from the plane."

"Nicolo." Aimee swallowed dryly. She had to find the right way to say this without sounding as if she was begging. "I've lived here all my life."

"And I," he said coolly, "have lived in Rome."

"Yes, I know that, but—"

"You are my wife."

His voice had turned hard; even the cabbie, sensing something, reached back and closed the privacy partition.

"But surely—"

"If you wish, I will consider the purchase of a flat in New York." Why tell her he'd decided on that when he first became interested in buying SCB? "But my primary residence—our primary residence—will be *Roma*."

"But—but—"

"Stop sounding like a motorboat," Nicolo said impatiently. "You are my wife. You will behave as such, and you cannot do that from a distance of thirty-five hundred miles."

Aimee felt the blood drain from her head. "Nicolo. Please—"

"This discussion is at an end."

Nicolo folded his arms and turned his face to the window.

"What discussion?" Aimee said bitterly. "You don't discuss things, you make pronouncements."

He gave her one final, unyielding look. "Get used to it," he said.

After that, there was silence.

Hell.

Nicolo glowered as he stared blindly out the window.

He was certainly doing his best to prove Aimee right and be just what she had called him. A no-good bastard. A son of a bitch. He was sure she'd have used other names, far more colorful ones, if only she'd known them.

But what did she expect?

First she told him how much she hated him. Then she told him she'd marry him. Then she said he was never to touch her.

He was the one with a title but his wife had been a princess long before she'd met him. A Park Avenue princess, accustomed to giving orders and getting her own way.

And he had married her.

He must have been out of his mind! How in hell had he let it happen?

He'd come to his senses last night, realized he didn't have to marry this woman. He didn't need her grand-father's bank. He hadn't needed a child, either, but since one was on the way, he'd finally figured out that he could do the right thing for it without marrying its mother....

It.

Not much of a way to think about one's *bambino* but then, he didn't know the sex. Damn it, he didn't even know if it *was* his child.

What in hell had happened to him, to make him do something so impetuous as marrying Aimee? Just because she said the baby was his....

Why believe her? Anything was possible with a woman who screwed like a bunny and wouldn't even exchange names.

Except, he knew he was the father. Knew it in his bones, and to hell with how ridiculous that sounded. He knew it, that was all, and because he hadn't been fast enough on his feet this morning, now he was stuck with the consequences.

He glanced at Aimee, sitting stiff and silent in the corner of the taxi, as far from him as she could get.

I feel the same way about you, he wanted to tell her. *I'm no happier about what we just did than you are. I don't want to look at you, talk to you, touch you...*

A lie.

He wanted to touch her, all right. Take her in his arms and kiss her until her lips were warm and softly swollen. Tear that demure-looking sundress off her body, bare her breasts to his eyes and mouth.

Bare her belly to his caress.

Her belly. Her womb. His child.

His child. That was why he'd married her. Of course it was. Why else would a man tie himself to a beautiful, hard-headed, ill-tempered woman he didn't know?

Nicolo glanced at Aimee again.

Why else, indeed?

He had phoned his pilot before the ceremony; when they reached the airport, the plane stood ready for departure.

He took Aimee's hand as they stepped out of the terminal. She didn't fight him. He almost wished she would. That might be better than letting her hand lie limply in his.

The pilot was already on board. The copilot and the cabin attendant were waiting on the tarmac, both of them smiling.

Nicolo had told them of his marriage.

"Congratulazioni, Principe, Principessa," the attendant said.

"Best of luck to you both," the copilot chimed in.

"Thank you," Nicolo replied.

Aimee said nothing.

Nicolo gritted his teeth. When they were alone in the cabin, he swung her toward him.

"I expect you to treat my people with courtesy!"

"What would you know of courtesy?" she said.

Their eyes met, hers daring him to ask her what she meant, but he knew better.

"Take a seat," he growled.

"Aren't you going to tell me what seat?"

Nicolo gritted his teeth again. At this rate, he would be toothless in a week.

"Do not test me, *cara*. I don't like it."

She smiled brightly, then sank into the first seat on the portside.

"Put the seat-back up."

She did.

"Close your safety belt."

She closed it.

"Damn it to hell, are you a robot?"

Aimee widened her eyes. "Isn't that what you want?"

He cursed, bent down and caught her chin in his hand. "I told you not to test me," he said with controlled rage in his voice. "Stop it now, or you will regret what happens next."

She jerked away from him. "I regret everything that's happened already. Why should I fear what happens next?"

Nicolo glared at her. He wanted to slap her. To kiss her. To throw her over his shoulder and carry her to the small bedroom in the rear of the cabin....

Was this what having a wife reduced a man to?

He looked at the seat next to hers. "I already do," he said coldly, and walked to the last seat on the starboard side and buckled himself in.

Moments later, they were skyborne.

Once they'd reached cruising altitude, Nicolo used the plane's satellite phone to call James Black.

At first, the old man didn't believe him.

"Married? Impossible," he scoffed. "There are laws. No one can get married so quickly."

"Aimee and I are married," Nicolo said coldly. And then, because he couldn't contain the words, "I expected you to be delighted by the information, *signore*. After all, it was part of your plan."

"An excellent plan, Your Highness, as I'm sure you now agree."

"There is more."

"Of course. The papers, transferring ownership of the bank to you. I'll start the procedure tomorrow."

Nicolo ran a hand through his hair. Amazing. He'd just told Black his granddaughter was married and all the old man could think about was his damnable bank.

"As I said, Signore Black, there is more."

"More?"

Suddenly Nicolo didn't want Black to know about Aimee's pregnancy. The baby was a private matter, not another thing over which the old man could gloat. Let him think the acquisition of the bank was the reason for the marriage.

"*Mi dispiace, signore.* A, um, a detail I just thought of but we can let the lawyers handle it."

"Then, I'll get my people to work immediately. Where shall they send the documents? To your attorney? Your office? It shouldn't take more than a week. Two, at the most. Are you at the hotel you were at before?"

"I have left the city, Signore Black. I—that is, we—are en route to my home in Rome."

"Excellent. I'll give instructions to forward the documents to you there. Goodbye, Your Highness."

Click. End of conversation. Nicolo was holding a dead phone.

Black hadn't inquired after Aimee. He hadn't asked to speak to her.

Nicolo put the phone aside. As far as her grandfather was concerned, Aimee was a gambit in an intricate business maneuver.

At least the old man would not be able to use her anymore.

He looked at the front of the plane. At Aimee, at his wife, who sat so rigidly in her seat. What was she thinking? In less than two days, her world had turned upside down.

Her grandfather had all but told her that her only value was as a lure. She'd learned she was pregnant. She had been coerced into marriage.

And yet, she remained proud. Strong. Defiant.

Nicolo imagined going to her. Taking her in his arms. Telling her that everything would be all right, that she could trust him to take care of her, that he—that he—

That he what?

He had used her, too. He'd wanted the bank and now he had it.

Nicolo put back his seat, shut his eyes and did his damnedest not to think.

An hour out of New York, the attendant, a pleasant young woman who'd been with him for several years, appeared with a bottle of Dom Pérignon and a pair of flutes.

"I hope you don't mind, sir," she began, "but we all thought…" She fell silent, her eyebrows reaching for the sky as she took in the seating arrangements.

"Thank you," Nicolo said quickly, "but my wife is exhausted and I didn't want to disturb her. Perhaps we'll have the champagne later."

"Of course, sir."

He smiled. Or hoped the way he curved his lips at least resembled a smile. Had he actually just explained himself to an employee? He didn't explain himself to anyone, ever.

"If we change our minds," he said, still straining to sound polite, "I'll ring."

The attendant knew a dismissal when she heard one. "Yes, sir," she said, and started back toward the cockpit.

Aimee stopped her.

"Wait," he heard her say.

The attendant leaned over the seat, listened, then smiled.

"That's very kind of you, *Principessa. Grazie.*"

Nicolo waited a few minutes after the attendant left. Then he walked up the aisle and took the seat next to Aimee's. Her face was turned to the window.

"Are you awake?"

The truth was he didn't give a damn one way or the other. He was tired of her silence, her coldness, of the way she'd made him look foolish during the ceremony and again now.

It was time he made things clear.

She was his wife. She would treat him with respect at all times.

"Did you really think I could sleep?"

"Your behavior continues to be unacceptable."

She looked at him then and the despair he saw in her eyes was like a knife to the heart.

That pain, knowing that she held him solely responsible for it, made him even more angry.

"Perhaps you didn't hear me," she said, as politely as she might speak to a servant. "I apologized."

"Perhaps you whispered your apology," he said coldly, "because I didn't hear it."

"I meant that I apologized to Barbara. The cabin attendant. It was sweet of her to bring champagne and I wanted her to know I hadn't meant to be rude. You were right. There's no reason for me to be discourteous to those who work for you."

He could almost hear the part she left unsaid, that there was every reason to be discourteous to him.

In the name of all the saints!

All right. He had to calm himself. Not take every word, every intonation, as a personal affront. She was his wife; they had to find a way to make the best of things.

He would offer a conciliatory gesture.

"Well, that was generous of you." He hesitated. "Would you like to join me for dinner?"

She turned her face to the window. "I'm not hungry."

"It's another three hours until—"

"I said, I'm not hungry."

So much for conciliatory gestures. And that tone of voice! When had she begun using it? Did she know what an insult it was, to be spoken to that way?

She had surely grown up with servants and after watching how she'd just dealt with Barbara, he'd damned well bet she'd never treated an employee or a servant as she was treating him.

If he'd whisked her away from a life of deprivation, she might behave differently....

What an ugly thing to think!

Still, she might at least show some interest in him. In her new life. In where he was taking her.

He didn't know why that should matter, but it did.

"I live in Rome," he said, after the silence became too much. "In the oldest part of the city. The *palazzo's* been in my family for centuries, but it wasn't in very good repair until I—"

"I don't care."

Nicolo didn't think. He reacted. Grabbed her, hauled her out of her seat and onto his lap. She started to scream and he captured her mouth with his, thrust his tongue between her lips, slipped his hands under her skirt.

She bit him. Beat at his shoulders with her fists. It didn't stop him. Nothing would. He had taken enough.

Her panties tore in half and she cried out, the sound muffled by his kiss.

"Such a lady you are now, *cara,*" he said against her mouth. "Such an elegant, bloodless gentlewoman with everyone except me."

"Nicolo. If you do this—"

"You'll what? Scream? Go ahead. You'll only embarrass yourself. I am Nicolo Barbieri. The sooner you learn what that means, the better."

He kissed her again and again, his hand moving against her flesh under her yellow skirt, cupping her, touching her, hating himself for what he was doing, hating her for what she had reduced him to, wanting what had happened between them that first night, that magical night, to happen again….

But not like this.

His kiss softened.

The stroke of his fingers became tender. He whispered Aimee's name between gentle kisses and all at once, she sighed against his mouth.

Her arms went around his neck.

Her lips parted beneath his.

And the petals of the sweetly feminine bud between her thighs began to bloom, the dew of it sweet and welcome against his palm.

Nicolo groaned. Shifted Aimee so that she was straddling him. Reached for his zipper...

And realized that even as she kissed him, his wife was weeping. Weeping as if her heart might break.

Nicolo went still. Then he groaned, though not with desire, and folded her into his arms.

"Don't cry," he murmured. "Please, *il mio amante,* don't cry."

He whispered to her, soft English words giving way to softer ones in Italian as he rocked her gently against his heart and stroked her honey-colored curls back from her face.

Gradually Aimee's sobs faded. She sighed deeply; he felt her breathing slow.

And knew she was asleep. Asleep, in his arms.

Nicolo sat without moving, his heart filled with a sweet, soaring emotion. Tenderness, he thought in surprise.

Tenderness.

Time slipped by. Finally, carefully, he depressed the button that reclined the leather seat. He lay back, drew Aimee even closer until she was lying in his arms, her body softly pressed against his, this woman fate had brought into his life.

This wife he hadn't wanted. This wife he didn't want...

She sighed, curved her arm around his neck. He felt the warmth of her breath, the warmth of her.

Something shifted inside him.

Nicolo closed his eyes and buried his face in Aimee's hair. He held her that way until he knew they were on their approach to Rome.

Then, carefully, he eased his arms from around his

sleeping wife, rose and went back to his seat in the rear of the cabin.

It was a lot safer than staying where he was.

CHAPTER TEN

SOMEONE was gently shaking Aimee's shoulder. She came awake slowly, lips curved in a hesitant smile.

"Nicolo?" she whispered.

"No, *Principessa. Scusi.*" The attendant smiled in apology. "The prince is in the rear of the cabin. Shall I get him for you?"

"No!" Flustered, Aimee sat up and ran her hands through her sleep-tangled curls. "That won't be necessary."

"I'm sorry to disturb you, but we'll be on the ground in a few minutes. Safety regulations require you to fasten your seat belt and return your seat to an upright position."

"Of course. Thank you."

The flight attendant nodded and made her way to the cockpit. Alone again, Aimee checked her watch. Had she really slept for most of the flight? It was too long a time; it had left her feeling groggy.

She always reacted that way to transatlantic flights. Groggy. Disoriented...

Had she dreamed of being in Nicolo's arms? Dreamed he'd begun to make love to her?

She had responded. God, yes, she'd responded....

And started to weep, knowing it was wrong. Wrong to want him, to need him, to yearn for his possession.

"Shh," he'd murmured, going from passion to tenderness in a heartbeat, holding her close, rocking her in his arms, promising that she had nothing to fear, that he would always take care of her...

It had to have been a dream.

If Nicolo had tried to make love to her, she wouldn't have let him. And he'd never have been satisfied with simply holding her in his arms. He hadn't married her for that.

He'd married her for the bank. For the child in her womb.

For sex.

The plane gave a gentle lurch as the wheels touched the runway. Aimee undid her seat belt. By the time she rose to her feet, Nicolo was at her side. His hand closed around her elbow.

"Thank you," she said politely, "but I'm perfectly capable of managing on my own."

"Are you always this gracious, *cara,* or is it something you reserve for me?"

Aimee jerked away from him and walked to the door. The pilot and copilot smiled and touched their hats.

"Buona notte, Principessa."

Principessa. That was who she was now. Was the title supposed to make up for the loss of her independence?

She forced a smile, wished them a good evening, too, and went down the steps to the tarmac.

It was night. She'd known it would be; still, the sense of disorientation swept over her again. She must have swayed. Stumbled. Something, because Nicolo gave an impatient snort and put his arm around her waist.

"I said—"

"I know what you said." He drew her close and led her toward a black Mercedes that waited a few yards away, a uniformed driver standing rigidly beside it. At their approach, he snapped his heels together, saluted and opened the rear door.

Apparently the sight of his employer half carrying a woman through the night was not unusual.

"Sede benvenuta, Principe."

"Grazie, Giorgio. Aimee, this is my driver. Giorgio, this is *mia moglie.* My wife."

Giorgio touched his cap again. *"Principessa,"* he said, but he didn't so much as blink.

Why would he? Nicolo wasn't just his boss, he was of royal blood. In America, especially in Manhattan, royals were just another species of celebrity. The gossip columns gushed over their doings but real people, New York people, hardly took notice.

This was not New York.

This was Rome. Nicolo's turf. It meant something here, to be known as a prince.

Aimee shuddered. In that single moment, she finally understood what had happened to her.

She'd left more than her old life behind. She'd left who she was—and who she might have been.

Her husband was everything she'd fought against all her life, and she was all but helpless to fight his demands... though he'd learn soon enough that she'd damned well die trying.

And for all of that, she still melted when he touched her.

Aimee's heart began to race. She wasn't ready for this! No one could be. So many changes, so many pages torn out and discarded from the life she'd planned for herself...

She began to tremble and despised herself for it but the more she tried to stop, the more she shook. She tried covering it with a flippant remark about the great Prince Barbieri being too important to have bothered with Customs.

Nicolo wasn't buying it.

"Are you ill?"

"I'm fine."

Her teeth, clicking like castanets, spoiled the lie. Nicolo muttered something, put his arms around her and drew her into his lap.

"Don't," she said, but he ignored her, drew her closer until she was encased in his warmth.

She tried to sit up straight, even now that she was in his lap, but it was impossible. For one thing, she felt silly, perched like that.

For another, he wouldn't permit it. His arms tightened around her and he gathered her closer to him.

"Stop being foolish," he said sternly. "I am not about to sit here and listen to your teeth chatter."

Finally she gave up fighting and lay back in his arms. As soon as she did, she knew it was what she wanted to do, despite her protests.

Though it made no sense, being in Nicolo's arms made her feel safe.

They rode in a silence broken only by the soft purr of the car's engine through the dark, winding streets of a sleeping Rome.

After a while, Aimee realized the Mercedes was climbing a hill.

"The Pallatine," Nicolo said, as if he'd read her mind. "My home—our home—is on its crest."

Ahead, a high gate swung slowly open. The car moved through it, then along a straight, narrow road that lay like a ribbon of black velvet. Tall Roman pines on either side blocked out the sky.

Suddenly a building loomed up before them.

"The Palazzo Barbieri," Nicolo said softly. "It has been in our family since the time of Caesar."

The night was too dark, the *palazzo* still too far away to see clearly, but Aimee didn't have to see the details to know the palace would be a hulking, joyless paean to antiquity.

It would swallow her whole.

She shuddered, and Nicolo cupped her face and turned it to his.

"Cara," he said softly, "don't be afraid."

"I'm not," Aimee answered quickly, as if the lie might make it true. "I've never been afraid of anything in my life."

Nicolo looked at her defiant expression and thought it might be true. Or, at least, that she had learned, early, that showing fear could be dangerous.

It was a lesson he understood.

Courage, a show of it, anyway, was the conqueror of demons. It was how he had overcome poverty and, he suspected, how his wife had survived James Black's attempts to control her life and undermine her spirit.

His wife.

This beautiful, brave woman was his wife. Had he taken a moment to tell her he was proud to have made her his *principessa?* To tell her that he knew theirs was a rocky start but he would do his best to make her happy? To tell her—to tell her that he was not sorry he'd made her pregnant, because he wasn't. He wasn't. He—

"Principe Nicolo. Siamo arrivato."

Nicolo blinked. The car had stopped; Giorgio stood beside the open rear door, eyes straight ahead, back rigid, chauffeur's cap square on his head.

How many times had he told the man he didn't want him to show subservience or, even worse, to wear that ridiculous cap?

All right. Time to take a deep breath. This was becoming a habit, letting his anger at himself turn into anger at others.

He stepped from the car, Aimee still in his arms. She struggled; he tightened his grasp.

"Really, Nicolo, I'm all right now."

"Really, Aimee," he said in near-perfect imitation of her tone, "you are not all right. It is late, you are tired and you are with child."

She shot a look at the driver.

"Nicolo!"

"My wife is pregnant, Giorgio," Nicolo said, and started up the wide steps to the door of the *palazzo*.

A quick smile tugged at the driver's lips. Aimee felt her face flame.

"Shh," she hissed.

"Tomorrow, first thing, we shall see an OB-GIN."

"OB-GYN, and must you announce it to the world?"

"I should have thought of it sooner. *Dio*, for all I know, you should not have taken such a long flight."

"For goodness' sakes," she said, glaring at him, "I'm *pregnant*, not—"

Aimee heard a loud gasp. She looked around. The *palazzo* doors had swung open on an enormous entrance hall….

And she had made her announcement to six, God, to seven people, all of them staring at her and beaming.

"Buona notte," Nicolo said pleasantly. "Aimee. This is my staff."

He rattled off names and duties. A housekeeper. Two cooks. Three maids. A gardener. They curtsied, bowed, smiled. Aimee, trapped in Nicolo's arms, wishing the floor would open so she could drop through it, did her best to smile back.

"And this," he told the little assemblage, "is *mia moglie*. My wife."

A gasp. A giggle. A hand quickly clapped over a mouth.

"As she has already told you, she is pregnant with my child."

Aimee started to bury her face in his throat but the sound of his voice stopped her.

Since she'd told him she was pregnant, Nicolo had gone from disbelief to shock to a stern acceptance of responsibility.

Now—now, his words resonated with pride. He sounded like a man who was happy his woman was having his baby.

She tilted her face up to his. For a heartbeat, they looked deep into each other's eyes.

Then the staff of the Barbieri *palazzo* broke into wild applause.

Aimee blushed. Nicolo laughed and dropped a light kiss on her lips. Then he carried her up the stairs.

A sweet moment, she thought in surprise, after a day of darkness...

But it didn't last.

He carried her down the hall, through another pair of massive doors, put her on her feet...

And everything changed

They were in a bedroom. His bedroom. You didn't need a sign on the wall to tell you that.

The room was huge and handsome, assuming your idea of "handsome" involved a marble fireplace big enough for an ox roast flanked by a pair of burnished-by-time leather sofas, a—a *thing* on the wall that was surely a crossbow...

And a bed the size of Aimee's entire apartment back in Manhattan.

Nicolo had already shut the door and tossed his jacket on a chair. *Say something,* she thought, searched frantically for something clever and instead blurted, "This is your room."

He looked at her as if she were a not-terribly-bright five-year-old.

"How clever of you, *cara*."

She needed to be calm. After all, he'd been very civilized just a few minutes ago.

"And where—" She cleared her throat. "And where is mine? I told you—"

"My memory is excellent," he said coolly. His hands were at his belt buckle. "I know what you told me. That we would have—what is it called? A marriage of convenience."

"Yes. And you—" The belt fell open. "Must you do that?"

"Do what?"

"You're—you're undressing…."

He pulled his shirt over his head. Muscles rippled in his forearms and biceps. Don't look, she told herself, but only a fool would have averted her eyes from the wide shoulders, the silky covering of coal-black hair on his broad chest, the washboard abs, the burgeoning male beauty she knew made up the rest of him.

"*Si*. I am undressing. It's what I generally do when it's late and I'm tired." His eyes met hers. "And ready for bed."

Her knees turned to water. Her heartbeat accelerated. *Don't look. Don't answer. Don't let him draw you into this game.*

"Aren't you ready for bed, too, *cara?*" He came toward her, the look on his face more powerful than any aphrodisiac. Slowly he reached out, trailed a lazy finger the length of her throat. "Aimee," he said in a low, husky voice, "come to bed."

She stared at him, hypnotized by his words, his eyes, by the intensity of her own desire because she wanted him, wanted him, wanted him….

"No," she said in a choked whisper and fled past him, into the bathroom, slammed the door and locked it.

"Aimee."

Nicolo's fist pounded against the door. Aimee dragged in a sobbing breath and closed her eyes.

"Aimee. Open this door!"

She shook her head as if he could see her. She would not open it. She would never open it or give herself to him because if she did—if she did, he would have everything. The respect she'd never been able to wrest from her grand-father. The bank that should have been hers. The child he'd put in her belly…

And her.

Most of all, worst of all, he'd have her. Her body, her soul, her passion…

And what would remain of Aimee Black then? Nothing. She would disappear. Everything she'd worked so hard to be, the independent woman she was, would be consumed in the fire of their lovemaking.

But she could survive that.

She could thrive on it.

Oh, she could…if only what Nicolo felt for her was more than desire. If what he felt was—if what he felt was—

"Aimee, damn it!" The door shuddered under another blow. "When will you stop running? When will you admit what you want, what we both want?"

Never, she thought, never!

Another blow against the door. Not his fist this time. His shoulder. And the door swung open and banged against the tiled wall.

Aimee cried out. Jumped back, fists raised. She would fight him to keep him from dominating her.

"Damn you, Nicolo—"

"Perhaps," he said grimly, "but you are my wife. You

will do as I say. And what I say, tonight, is that I'm tired of you pretending you don't want me when we both know damned well you do."

He reached for her. Dragged her into his arms. She swung at him; he caught both her wrists, trapped her hands between them. Took her mouth…

And tasted not her anger but her tears, just as he had on the plane.

Dio, he thought. *Dio,* what was he doing?

"Aimee."

He tried to lift her face to his. She wouldn't let him.

"Aimee. *Mia cara…*"

The sound of her weeping was killing him. Nicolo cursed softly, swept his wife into his arms and held her close, his mouth against her temple.

"Don't cry," he whispered, "Aimee, *il mio tresoro,* I beg you, don't cry."

She was pregnant, ill and exhausted. And all he'd thought about was himself.

Slowly he gathered her to him. Rocked her against him. Pressed light kisses into her hair.

Little by little, her weeping stopped.

"Good girl," he said softly.

Nicolo stepped out of the bathroom and carried her to the bed. He sat down, his back against the silk pillows, his wife in his arms, his cheek pressed to the top of her head.

"Forgive me, *amante,*" he whispered. "You were very brave today and I have repaid that bravery with terror."

Aimee drew in a staggered breath. Nicolo reached to the night table, took a handful of tissues from a box and brought them to her nose.

"Blow," he said softly.

She did. The sound made him smile.

"Such a big sound for such a delicate female," he said.

"I'm not delicate."

He smiled again. Her voice was small but still, she couldn't let his throwaway remark pass without argument. The look of a tigress and the heart of one, as well.

"More tissues?"

Aimee shook her head.

"You sure? I'm getting good at this. Paper towels, tissues…who knows? Someday, I might even work up to a handkerchief."

Did her lips curve in a smile? He wanted to believe they had.

"Aimee." He tilted her face to his. This time, she let him do it. "*Cara,* I am sorry."

Nothing. Well, what had he expected? She hated him.

"It is something I do, this—this thing of making quick decisions, of not asking advice."

Not true. He made decisions that seemed quick but only after he'd done his homework. He didn't ask advice often but when he did, he respected the answers he received.

He was not a man given to impulse, especially in his private life. He'd seen too many men with money and power make spur-of-the-moment choices about women, and end up paying for it for the rest of their lives, financially and emotionally.

To give in to impulse was dangerous. A sure road to disaster. Emotion had no part in decision-making…

Except when it came to Aimee. To wanting her. Needing her. Desiring her, in his arms, his bed, his life…

Nicolo frowned.

Aimee was exhausted, but she wasn't the only one. So was he. Otherwise, he wouldn't be having such strange thoughts.

Carefully he eased her from his arms, onto the bed beside him, then rose to his feet.

"Sleep here tonight," he said carefully. "We can discuss our room arrangements tomorrow. Meanwhile, I'll ring for Anna. She'll help you undress and get to bed."

He looked down at his wife. Her hair was spread across the pillows—*his* pillows—in a wild, honey-soft tangle. Her face was still pale, her eyes glittered from the tears she'd shed, her mouth trembled....

And he knew that he wanted her for more than the child she carried, certainly for more than the bank her grandfather owned. He wanted her for reasons he couldn't understand and that made it all the more important to step back, walk away....

But he didn't.

Instead he took her hands in his.

"Or," he said gruffly, "I can undress you. I can put you to bed and lie with you, *cara.* Not to make love to you but to hold you in my arms as you sleep...and to promise you that I will honor you, care for you, that I will not frighten you again."

He wasn't sure what he expected her to say. Anything from "no" to "are you insane?" would probably have suited... But when she finally answered him, it was in a whisper so soft he had to bend his head to hear it.

"I—I feel safe when you hold me."

He swallowed. "You should, *cara.* After all, I am—I am your husband."

Their eyes met. Aimee smiled. Nicolo smiled back. Then he went to his closet and returned with a pair of burgundy-colored silk pajamas.

"Stand up," he said softly.

Aimee obeyed. Turned her back so he could unzip the yellow dress. Strip it from her. Under it, she wore only a scrap of white lace.

Nicolo swallowed again. Decided that leaving the bit

of lace would probably be the only intelligent thing to do, but why worry about intelligence?

A man who stripped a woman naked, then didn't touch her, had no claim on intelligence.

Carefully he hooked his thumbs in the panties. She gave a little gasp and he acted as if it were important that he was easing them down her hips, her long legs.

"Lift your foot. Now the other," he said and that gave him away. Was that thick, rough voice really his?

He tossed the scrap of lace aside. Rose to his feet. Did his best not to look at his wife but how could he not, when she was so exquisite? He had not seen her naked since the night they'd met but he remembered, oh, yes, he remembered….

Her body had changed. He would not have imagined it possible but it was even more beautiful now that she carried his baby. Her breasts were larger, her nipples darker. And her belly… Was he wrong, or was it just slightly fuller?

By all the saints, he was going to lose his sanity if he didn't cup her breasts, lift them to his lips and kiss them. Kneel before her, put his mouth to her belly, to her feminine delta…

Nicolo dropped the burgundy pajama top on the bed and turned his back. "There," he said briskly. "That's for you. I'll wear the bottoms. Okay?"

He sensed her nod of acquiescence; he was not fool enough to look at her to make sure. As it was, he was doing mental multiplication tables to try to keep from becoming erect.

He had promised all he'd do was hold her in his arms and that was what he would do.

Quickly he took off what remained of his own clothes, stepped into the PJ bottoms and tied them.

"Ready?"

"Ready," Aimee said softly.

A deep, deep breath. Then he swung around. Her sandals stood neatly beside the bed; her panties were on the night table.

She was under the blanket.

God was merciful, after all.

Nicolo forced a smile, lifted the covers and slid in beside her. For a moment, neither of them moved. Then he turned, and she turned, and suddenly she was in his arms.

She smelled of flowers.

Her skin was silky.

Her hair was soft.

Eight times three is twenty-four. Twenty-four times two is forty-eight. Forty-eight times two is ninety-six. Ninety-six times, Dio, *ninety-six times ninety-six is—is—*

Nicolo shut his eyes, gathered Aimee into his embrace. She sighed, her breath a susurration of sweet warmth against his throat.

Please, he thought, please, let her fall asleep quickly. Once she did, he'd get up, read a book. Do some work. Anything but lie here with Aimee in his arms because, of course, he would not sleep. This was too much. She was half-naked, they were completely alone...

He smiled.

And she had not called him a name in easily half an hour. That was a first.

It was a night of firsts. He'd never had a wife before, never even had a woman in this bed until now. He'd never slept with one without making love to her and most of all, most of all, he'd never held a woman against him and felt—and felt—

He drew back a little. Another minute, he'd carefully push back the covers, leave the bed—

"Nicolo?"

His wife's voice was soft as the touch of a feather.

"Yes, *cara?*"

"Did I fall asleep in your arms on the plane, or was it a dream?"

Nicolo brushed his lips lightly over hers. "It was not a dream, *amante*. You slept just like this…and I hated to leave you."

"I'm sorry you did," she whispered.

A second later, she was asleep.

Get up, Nicolo told himself, you damned fool, get out of this bed right now.

Instead he rolled onto his back, taking Aimee with him, her head nestled in the curve of his shoulder, her arm thrown lightly over his chest.

He stared up at the ceiling, at a tiny bit of moonlight caught in the ancient fresco of cherubs and fauns.

"Ninety-six times ninety-six," he whispered into the darkness, "is—is nine thousand two hundred and sixteen."

Then, to his amazement, he closed his eyes and slept.

CHAPTER ELEVEN

SOMETIME JUST before dawn, it began to rain.

The windows were all open; a breeze ruffled the curtains and brought with it the scent of the gardens that surrounded the *palazzo*.

Aimee was warm and safe in Nicolo's arms, her body sprawled half over his, hearts beating in unison.

She was asleep.

He was awake.

Awake, and enduring the sweetest kind of torture. The feel of her against him. The whisper of her breath against his naked shoulder. The gentle weight of her thigh over his.

Nicolo was trapped halfway between the heaven of holding his beautiful wife in his embrace and the hell of knowing he had promised he would not touch her.

It had seemed an easy promise to make.

Aimee was exhausted. She was pregnant. And he had no wish to risk the fragile peace that had sent her into his arms hours before by doing something foolish.

Except—except, he hadn't expected her to drape herself over him like this. To sigh so sweetly each time she shifted against him. He hadn't expected to want to wake her with his kisses, with his caresses, and tell her that somewhere between yesterday and today, he had gone from feeling like a man in a trap to a man who had—who had met his destiny.

A destiny he welcomed.

Nicolo frowned into the darkness.

How could that be? His life was perfect. The pauper prince had made himself one of the world's richest men. He was respected. Admired. He had everything a man could possibly want....

And now, he had more.

A child on the way. And a wife.

Aimee. Bright. Articulate. And exasperating. But *Dio*, what courage she had! Choosing a life she didn't want, a life that was the opposite of the one he knew she'd desired, because it was the right thing to do.

Aimee, who excited him more than any woman he'd known.

Was she his destiny?

Not that he believed in such things. A man was born into the world. Beyond that, the life he lived was his own. You made choices, walked a path you controlled.

Or maybe not.

Was there a force people called fate? Did it wait for the chance to scoop you up and put you on a different path? A path you'd never intended to follow?

Was that what had happened to him?

Two days ago, he'd been Nicolo Barbieri, prince of a royal house of Rome. A man who headed a financial empire. Who answered to no one.

Aimee sighed and burrowed closer.

Now, he was Nicolo Barbieri, husband and soon-to-be father. It was an impressive responsibility, one he surely hadn't planned or wanted....

And yet, it felt right. The baby in Aimee's womb. Aimee in his arms. In his bed.

Aimee, his bride. His wife. His—his—

Nicolo frowned. Carefully he eased his arm from her shoulders, his leg from beneath her thigh. He needed a cup of espresso. Or a walk around the garden. Or maybe he'd turn on his computer, check his e-mail. Yes. That was what he would do. In the confusion of the last few days, he'd damned near lost touch with his office.

He had never done that before.

He sat up, rose from the bed and ran his hands through his hair.

This was not good, this disruption in his life. He had a company to run, people who looked to him for direction. He had to get back on track. He would shower, turn on the computer. His housekeeper would be up soon; over a quick breakfast, he'd talk with her, ask her to explain the functions of his household to Aimee when she came down, arrange for Giorgio to drive her to whatever shops she wished. Oh, and he would contact his physician, ask him to recommend the best OB-GYN in Rome.

No more of this nonsense. Of putting everything aside just because he'd made a woman pregnant and married her—

"Nicolo?"

He swung around. Aimee was sitting up against the pillows. He could see her clearly in the rain-washed light of dawn. Her eyes filled with uncertainty. Her cascade of tousled curls. The outline of her breasts under his pajama top.

This was his wife. His woman. His Aimee.

Everything else flew out of his head. Something swept through him, an emotion so powerful it made his breath catch.

"Yes, *cara*," he said softly. Smiling, he went to the bed and sat down next to her. "I'm sorry. I didn't mean to wake you."

Aimee pushed her hair away from her eyes.

"I didn't mean to sleep so late."

"No, sweetheart, it isn't late at all. The sun's barely up. I just—I just couldn't sleep anymore."

"Jet lag," she said, with a little smile.

"*Si*," he said, because that was easier than explaining what had driven him from the bed.

And what had now brought him back to it.

"Go back to sleep, *cara*. You need your rest."

"No. No, I'm—I'm—" She went white. "Oh. Oh…"

She shot from the bed so quickly that he had only risen to his feet by the time she slammed the bathroom door after her.

"Go away," she gasped when he flung it open, and then she bent over the commode and retched.

Nicolo's heart turned over. He cupped her shoulders, steadied her until the spasm passed. Then he turned her in his arms, despite her protests.

"I will take you back to bed," he said firmly. "And you will stay there until the doctor arrives."

"I'm not sick. This is just a thing that happens to some women when they're pregnant." She looked up with a shaky smile. "I'll be fine once I wash up. You'll see."

She was right about the vomiting. He knew that much. He also knew that he'd been terrified, seeing her suffer.

"Nicolo. Please. Go away and let me clean up."

Aimee watched him consider the situation and wondered if this was how he looked in his office, so dark, determined and brooding. Finally he nodded curtly, took a new toothbrush from a drawer in the vanity, showed her where the towels were, the comb, the hairbrush….

"Nicolo," Aimee said gently. "I'll find everything on my own. I promise."

She had to swear she would call him if she felt ill, that

she wouldn't lock the door so he could reach her quickly if necessary.

Finally she was alone.

She showered. Washed her hair, brushed her teeth, wrapped herself in a huge towel....

And tried not to think about the man waiting in the next room.

Her husband.

She had slept in his arms all night. Close to him. Warmed by him. Comforted by his presence.

She'd also been awake when he'd awakened this morning.

She'd wanted to tell him that, but she'd been mortified to find herself draped half over him. Besides, what did you say to your husband when you didn't know him?

Good morning didn't seem to cut it.

Especially when what you really wanted to do—what you *really* wanted was not to say a word but to clasp his face, bring his mouth to yours, kiss him and tell him that you'd changed your mind, you didn't want to be his wife in name only....

Aimee shut her eyes. Took a deep breath. Opened the door. With luck, Nicolo would have dressed and gone by now....

He hadn't.

He was standing in the middle of the room, bare-chested, arms folded, eyes almost black as he looked at her.

"Are you better?"

She nodded. "I'm fine."

His gaze swept over her. The towel was big but that gaze made her feel naked.

"We will see a physician today."

"Really, I'm—"

"You're beautiful."

His voice was husky. The sound of it, that look in his eyes, made her heart turn over.

"No. I mean, I haven't dried my hair. And I'm already gaining weight. And—"

"Where is this weight?"

"My breasts. My belly. Not much, but—"

"I want to see."

A heavy silence descended on the room. Aimee's eyes met Nicolo's.

"I want to see the changes my child has made in you," he said softly as he started toward her. He stopped inches away, his hands now at his sides, his eyes hot on hers. "Let me look at you."

"Nicolo." Her tongue felt thick. She swallowed, swallowed again. "I don't think—"

"That's right. Don't think." He reached out, grasped the edge of the towel she clutched to her breasts. "It is a husband's right to see his wife." And before she could muster a shield of anger at that bit of arrogance, he added a single word that left her defenseless. "Please."

Aimee took a deep breath. Then, slowly, she let go of the towel.

For what seemed an eternity, Nicolo stood still. Didn't touch her. Didn't do anything but sweep his eyes over her nakedness.

Then he cupped her breasts. Feathered his thumbs over her nipples. Ran his hand down her ribs and over her belly.

He looked up at her, and what she saw in his face made her heartbeat stumble.

"Aimee," he said thickly, "my wife. My beautiful, amazing wife…"

The next instant, she was in his arms.

He kissed her hungrily and she returned his kiss. Her arms wound around his neck as he carried her to the bed and lay her down among the sheets of softest Egyptian cotton.

He kissed her hair, her temple, her throat. Her soft moans, the way she lifted herself to him, stoked the flames he'd tried so hard to control.

He told himself he would be gentle. She was pregnant. She'd been ill. She needed tenderness, not the fire that burned within him....

And then her lips parted. The tip of her tongue stroked into his mouth—and Nicolo was lost.

He bent to her breasts, sucked the nipples deep into his mouth. Aimee cried out, arched toward him and it was all he could do not to part her thighs and bury himself inside her.

She tasted of honey. Of cream. Of all the delicacies in the universe. He loved the sweetness of her skin, the tang of salt as it began to heat under his caresses.

He loved everything about this. About her. The way she responded to him, without holding anything back.

That first night, their coming together had been wild, almost savage, but now he realized she'd let him be the aggressor.

Now, she was the one, telling him with every motion, every sigh, that she wanted him. Wanted this. Wanted all he could give her and more.

Her hands explored his shoulders. His chest. She kissed his throat, touched her tongue to the hollow where he knew his heart must be racing.

"Nicolo," she whispered, and her fingers brushed the tip of his straining erection.

He let her explore him, loving her touch, her caution, her, yes, her innocence, but when her hand closed around him, he knew it was time to take control of her and of himself.

"No," he said roughly and caught her wrists, pinned them high over her head, held her captive to his lips, his teeth, his kisses until she was sobbing with need.

"Please," she whispered, "please…"

Nicolo tore off his pajama bottoms, kicked them away. Knelt between his wife's thighs and kissed that tender flesh. She cried out, arched to him again and he brushed the back of his hand over the honey-colored curls that guarded her femininity.

Aimee cried out. Bucked under him and he caught her wrists again, this time in one hand, and used the other to touch her.

She was wet.

Fragrant with arousal.

She was sobbing. Pleading. And he—he was going to explode if he didn't take her soon.

Her clitoris was swollen with passion and when he finally let go of her wrists, slipped his hands under her bottom and brought her to his mouth, her taste was exquisite.

Aimee cried out and he moved up her body, spread her thighs wide and she wrapped her legs around his hips.

"Now," he said, and entered her on a long, hard thrust.

Her cry was high and sweet and all he had ever yearned for. He surged forward again and she screamed, flung her head back and came apart in his arms again and again as he held her, as he caught her mouth with his and drank in her sobs.

"Nico," she whispered against his mouth and he shot over the edge, let go of who he was, who he had been, all of it lost in the warm, welcoming body of his wife.

A lifetime later, Nicolo stirred. Aimee was still beneath him and he began to roll away from her, but she put her arms around him and held him close.

"Stay," she whispered.

He wanted to. He would stay like this forever, if he could.

"I'm too heavy for you, *cara mia*."

"I don't care."

She sounded so determined, it made him smile.

"Let's try reversing things." He rolled onto his back and took her with him so that she was sprawled on top of him. "How's that?"

She gave the kind of long sigh that reached straight into his heart.

"It's wonderful."

Oh, it was. More than wonderful, he thought, wrapping his arms even more tightly around her. They lay that way for a few minutes, until his heartbeat and hers had slowed. Then he cupped the back of her head and brought her mouth to his for a tender kiss.

"Are you all right?" he said softly.

Her lips curved against his. "I'm very all right."

Nicolo grinned. "I agree completely, *Principessa*. In fact…" Another kiss, longer than the last. "You are wonderfully all right.

"I liked what you called me," he said, stroking the curls back from her face.

Aimee propped her chin on her hands. "What I called you?"

"*Si*. Nico." He smiled. "No one ever called me Nico before."

"Never?"

"Never. My governesses always referred to me as *Principe*." He chuckled. "Except for one daring Englishwoman who called me Master Nicolo."

"Were there many governesses?"

He nodded. "My parents were always traveling. My

great-grandmother lived with us but she was already very old when I was born, so I was raised by governesses. And whenever my parents came home, they'd find fault with the governess of the moment and fire her."

"They were that awful?"

"Some were better than others but none were 'awful.'"

"Then, why?"

Nicolo sighed. "It took me a while to figure it out but I finally realized it was jealousy. My mother would see my attachment to a governess and that was the kiss of death."

Aimee framed his face between her hands.

"If your mother wanted you to love her, why didn't she stay home and take care of you herself?"

"It was just the way they were, *cara,* she and my father. Their lives were all about self-gratification. No responsibility. No money, either. The *palazzo* was falling down around my ears by the time I inherited it—but that was how they lived, on their titles and the largesse of their friends."

"And now?"

Nicolo lifted his mouth to hers for a kiss. "And now, *amante mia,* it no longer matters. They are both gone. A plane, taking them to a polo match in Palm Springs…"

"Oh, I'm sorry."

"It's all right, sweetheart. To tell the truth, I didn't know them well enough to miss them."

"A child shouldn't grow up that way."

The fervor in her voice made him smile.

"No. I agree." He stroked his hand down her back. "And you, *cara?* How was life with James Black… Or do I not have to ask?"

Aimee sighed. "He took me in when my parents died. I'll always be grateful to him for that. I was very little, you see, and there was no money… My father had married a woman Grandfather didn't find suitable, and…"

"And," Nicolo said, trying to control his sudden anger, "he did his best to make your father pay for it and to hell with how it affected you or your mother."

There was a time Aimee would have defended her grandfather. She'd have said he'd done what he thought was right, but now she'd married a man who had done what he thought was right and it had nothing to do with what he'd wanted for himself but only with what he wanted for others.

For her and their unborn child.

"Yes," she said softly, "he didn't care about anyone but himself. But my parents were happy, Nicolo. They adored each other and they adored me. I loved them so much and then—and then they died and I went to live with Grandfather, and—and—" She gave a sad little laugh that almost broke his heart. "There he was, stuck with the child of a woman he'd never acknowledged. A girl child, at that."

"I'm sure he didn't hide his disappointment," Nicolo said, his voice harsh.

"I wasn't what he wanted. I had no desire to learn to become the perfect wife to his idea of the perfect husband."

"A man he'd choose," Nicolo said, rolling her beneath him. "A captain of industry, with blood as blue as your grandfather's."

Aimee ran her fingers through Nicolo's tousled black curls. "Were you listening to all those conversations?" she said with a little smile.

"A man who could control you, as he had not been able to do."

Her smile faded. How quickly he'd understood. "Yes."

"And who would love Stafford-Coleridge-Black more than he loved you."

Aimee tried to look away. Nicolo wouldn't let her. He

caught her face between his palms and held it steady under his gaze. Her eyes glittered, but she forced a smile.

"And he got what he wanted," she said lightly, "from the blue blood all the way to Stafford-Coleridge-Bl—"

Nicolo silenced her with a deep, passionate kiss.

"I married you," he said fiercely, "not your grandfather's financial empire."

"It's all right. You don't have to try to make it sound as if—as if—"

"I married you because you carry my child. And because you are a strong, beautiful, fascinating woman."

"Please." Her voice trembled. "You don't have to lie."

"No lies, *cara*. Not now, not ever. Do you really think I'd have married you to get my hands on that damned bank?"

Even as he spoke the words, he knew they were true. He had married Aimee because she was going to bear his child, and because—because—

Because what? The answer was tantalizingly close.

For now, all he could come up with was the way to prove to his wife that he wanted her.

"Tomorrow," he said, "I will contact your grandfather. I will tell him that I do not want his bank."

"But you *do* want it! I won't let you do that for me."

"I am doing it for me, *cara*. Because—because I am— I am happy." He saw the smile that lit his bride's face and his heart seemed to expand within his chest. "I am very happy," he said softly, "and it has nothing to do with your grandfather's bank." Nicolo shifted his weight so Aimee could feel what lying against her had done to him. "I'm happy because of this," he whispered. "My child in your womb. And you, *anima mia,* forever in my arms."

"What does that mean? *Anima mia?*"

He smiled. "It means that you are my soul."

Tears glittered on Aimee's lashes. Was it possible to go from despair to joy so quickly?

The answer came a heartbeat later, when Nicolo slid deep inside her. Yes. Oh, yes, it was possible.

"Nico," Aimee whispered, "Nico…"

Then, for a very long time, there was no sound but the gentle patter of the rain and the softness of the lovers' sighs.

CHAPTER TWELVE

"BUON GIORNO, cara mia."

Nicolo's soft voice was the first thing Aimee heard as she awakened. She was lying close to him; he was on his belly, smiling down at her as her eyes fluttered open.

Her heart turned over. What a perfect start to a new day. To a new life.

"Buon giorno, Nicolo," she said softly.

She almost laughed at the look on his face. "You speak Italian?"

"Of course," she said, as if there could be no question about it. *"Buon giorno. Buono notte. Grazie. Per favore.* Oh, and, of course, *espresso, cappuccino,* and, um, *gelato."* She grinned. "See? All the essentials. Good morning. Good evening. Thank you, please, two kinds of coffee and the best ice cream in the world. How's that for speaking the language?"

Nicolo grinned back at her. "Ah. A high school trip to Italy."

"A Miss Benton's Academy trip to Five Famed Cities of Europe, if you please." She touched the tip of her finger to his lips, smiling when he caught it between his teeth and took a mock ferocious bite. "Twelve very proper young women, three even more proper chaperones, five cities, fifteen days." She rolled her eyes. "Truly memorable, but not in the way Miss Benton would have preferred. Evelyn got sick from too much onion soup in Paris, Louise sneaked ouzo into her room in Athens and got snockered—"

"Snockered?"

"The only slang word Miss Benton would have permitted as a descriptive," Aimee said primly, laughter dancing in her eyes.

"And you, *cara?* Did you dine on too much soup? Did you get snickered—"

"Snockered."

"*Si.* Did you get snockered on ouzo?"

"I behaved like the obedient little girl I was." Aimee's smile slipped a notch. "Not that it mattered."

"You mean, your grandfather still paid you no attention," Nicolo said, wrapping her in his arms as he rolled onto his side.

"I mean, obedient or not, I was still the wrong sex for a Black grandchild."

Nicolo wanted to rise from the bed, fly to the States and grab the old man by the collar, hoist him to his toes and tell him what a selfish, stupid, coldhearted SOB he was....

Instead he did the next best thing.

"I think you're the perfect sex," he murmured, and ran his hand slowly down her body.

She smiled, as he'd hoped she would.

"Mmm. Right now, I think so, too."

"So, aside from being a good girl, what were you like when you were a teenager?"

"Shy. Quiet. Skinny as a stick."

He caressed her again. "Seems to me you've grown up since then."

That won him another smile. *"Grazie."*

"Would you like to learn more Italian?"

Aimee wound her arms around his neck. "For instance?"

"Sei molto bella."

"Which means?"

"It means, you are very beautiful." Nicolo's voice grew husky. "Incredibly beautiful, *cara.*"

"Grazie."

"Wrong answer."

Her eyebrows rose. "Thank you is the wrong answer?"

He nodded. "Well, what should I have said in response?"

"You should have said, *Baciami,* Nico, *per favore.*"

Her lips curved. She'd caught on to the game.

"Baciami, Nico, *per favore,"* she said softly.

"With pleasure," he whispered, and kissed her.

Another kiss. And another, kisses that grew deeper and longer until Nicolo knew that soon, there'd be no turning back.

He groaned, kissed her one last time and rolled onto his back. Aimee made a sound of protest that went straight to his heart, and he gathered her closely against his side.

"We have things to do this morning."

"More important than this?"

"Nothing is more important than this... Except, perhaps, our ten o'clock appointment with Dr. Scarantino."

She rose up on her elbow. "Who?"

"I spoke with my physician about a doctor for you and the baby."

"Already?"

"I made the call hours ago," he teased, "while you lazed in bed."

"And why was I lazing in bed, do you think?"

Nicolo's eyes darkened. "If I answer that question, we'll miss our appointment with the best OB-GIN in all of *Roma.*"

Aimee brushed a lock of dark hair from her husband's forehead. She smiled, loving the way he mangled the abbreviation.

"After that, we'll stroll along the Via Condotti. Do you like Armani, *cara?* Valentino?" He smiled. "Who are your favorite designers, hmm? Tell me, and we will visit their shops today."

Her favorite designers were whatever was on sale in SoHo. Not taking money from her grandfather had long ago become a way of life.

"Nicolo. I brought a suitcase. I don't need—"

"And," he said, "then a stop at Bulgari for a proper wedding band. One that fits you and will tell the world that you are mine." He paused; his expression grew serious. "I did something else this morning, as well. I sent a fax to your grandfather, informing him that I do not wish to purchase his bank."

"No. I've thought about that. And I can't let you—"

"The choice is mine, *cara.* And I have already made it."

The words were arrogant, masculine…and wonderful. Aimee sighed and lay her head against her husband's shoulder.

"You are enough for me, Aimee. Do you understand?"

Was she enough? She had to believe it. Nicolo had sacrificed ownership of her grandfather's financial empire for her.

"Do you understand?" he said, rolling her onto her back.

"Yes," she said, "yes…"

He kissed her. Kissed her again… And forgot everything but making love to his wife.

A prince and his princess could surely be a few minutes late for an appointment.

* * *

The obstetrician—not an OB-G-Anything but *uno medico l'ostetrico*—was middle-aged, pleasant and, to Aimee's relief, spoke excellent English.

His calm demeanor was just what Nicolo needed.

Somehow, finding himself waiting in the doctor's private office while Aimee was examined had turned him from a man whose wife was having a baby into one whose wife was about to do something no female on the planet had ever done before.

He sprang to his feet when she and the doctor reappeared.

"*Cara.* Are you all right?"

"Yes. Of course. I'm—"

"Doctor? Is my wife well?"

"She is fine, *Principe.*"

"The baby, too?"

"The baby, too."

"You are sure?"

The doctor smiled. "I am sure."

"And what must we do to keep things that way?"

"The usual, *Principe.* A healthful diet. Exercise. No caffeine, no cigarettes."

"That's it?"

The doctor spread his arms wide. "*Si.* That is it."

Nicolo cleared his throat, the memories of the night and the morning suddenly vivid.

"And, ah, and what of, ah, what of restrictions on, ah, on her activities?"

Aimee blushed. The doctor hid a grin. "If you refer to sex—"

"*Si.*"

"Sex is a perfectly healthy activity."

Nicolo clasped Aimee's hand. "What else should we know?"

"In a few weeks, we will do some tests—we do them

for all pregnant women," the doctor added quickly, when Nicolo paled. "It is, how does one say it? Pro forma. Ultrasound. Blood work. Nothing out of the ordinary."

"You are sure?"

"I am quite sure."

Moments later, on the sidewalk, Aimee stopped and turned to Nicolo.

"I didn't want to embarrass you in front of the doctor," she said quietly, "but—but if you wish, they could do an additional test. For DNA. To prove to you that this baby is—"

Nicolo drew her close and silenced her with a kiss. "There is nothing you need prove to me, *cara*," he murmured. "We have agreed to tell each other only the truth, *si?*"

"*Si.* Yes. But if—"

"No lies," he said softly. "Not between us. Not ever."

He bought her more clothes than she could wear in a lifetime and when she whispered that it was a waste of money because, soon, she wouldn't fit into any of them, he held a quiet conversation with one of the shop assistants, who looked at Aimee and smiled.

"We will take all this," Nicolo said, gesturing to the stacks of trousers and sweaters, dresses and gowns Aimee had tried on.

Then he whisked her back into his car, to an elegant boutique that specialized in fashions for expectant mothers.

"I'll never wear all these things," Aimee said as the new pile of garments grew larger.

"I want you to have them," Nicolo said.

A pronouncement, not a suggestion. That was how her

husband faced the world, with authority and determination.

How he had now faced her grandfather because he wanted her, not Stafford-Coleridge-Black.

It seemed impossible. Nicolo's trips to the States. His meetings with James. He'd wanted the bank that same way, with authority and determination.

Not enough to marry her, of course…

But he *had* married her, because it was, he'd said, the right thing to do, once he knew she carried his heir.

In other words, he'd met James's conditions of sale.

Why insist on turning his back on the deal now?

For her. Only for her, Aimee thought, and something wonderful and just a little bit terrifying stirred in her heart.

At Bulgari, they looked at platinum wedding bands. For men as well as women because, Nicolo said, a husband should wear a ring as well as a wife.

Such a simple statement but it filled Aimee with joy.

Was it really only yesterday she'd stood before a judge, her heart cold as she took vows that bound her to this man?

Her heart was anything but cold now.

"Aimee?"

She looked up. Nicolo was watching her, a little smile on his face.

"What are you thinking, *cara?*" he said softly.

That I was wrong about you, my husband. That you are a kind, generous, wonderful man….

Not even she was foolish enough to bare her soul so quickly.

"I was thinking that—that it's going to be hard to choose rings when they're all so beautiful."

"Then let me simplify things and—"

"Nicolo," she said quickly, "are you sure you don't want the bank?"

He looked at her as if she'd gone crazy. "Didn't you ask me that a little while ago?"

"But—"

"But what? I gave you my answer. There are other banks." His smile tilted. "Besides, this particular bank should only have gone to you."

"It couldn't. My grandfather—"

Nicolo silenced her with a kiss.

"Now," he said softly, leaning his forehead against hers, "as to selecting rings… It's a warm day. You have been on your feet too long."

"I haven't. I sat in the car, sat at those shops, sat here—"

"There's a little café just down the street. Giorgio will drive you there."

"Giorgio will not drive me just down the street!"

"Fine. Then you will walk there, take an umbrella table, order espresso for me and a lemonade for you."

Aimee shook her head. "I think I've just been had!"

Nicolo gave her the kind of grin that made her blush.

"As soon as we get home, *cara*," he whispered, "I promise. For now, wait for me at the café." He paused. "Please."

How could she resist after that? Aimee rose on her toes and pressed a light kiss to her husband's mouth.

The café was crowded but she found a table shaded by a bright yellow Cinzano umbrella, dutifully ordered Nicolo's espresso and her cool drink, and waited.

Moments later, she saw him coming toward her. She began to smile—but the smile turned to astonishment.

"Nicolo! What are you doing?"

A silly question. He had dropped to his knees before

her. That not only got her attention, but it got everyone else's.

He took a small box from his pocket, opened it and revealed a ring that shone with all the fire an exquisitely set ten carat diamond could provide.

"Aimee," he said softly, "I know I should have asked you this question yesterday but the old saying says it is never too late to do the right thing." He took her hand and slipped the ring on her finger. "Will you be my wife?"

Tears filled Aimee's eyes. "Yes," she said, laughing and crying at the same time. "Oh, yes, Nico, yes, yes, yes—"

The café filled with cheers as she flung her arms around his neck and kissed him.

And, just that quickly, she knew the shocking truth.

She was deeply, passionately in love with her husband.

He had bought wedding bands, too, of course.

A wide one set with diamonds for her, a more austere version of the same ring for himself.

Still, even several weeks later, Aimee would catch sight of the solitaire and the wedding band glittering on her left hand and wonder how all this could have happened.

Didn't it take time to fall in love? Didn't you have to get to know a person? His likes, his dislikes. His favorite foods, his favorite movies, all that and more.

She and Nicolo were still learning those things but none of them seemed terribly important.

One look into her husband's eyes in that café and she'd tumbled straight off the edge of the earth.

Or maybe it had happened when they met. Maybe what she'd experienced in Nicolo's arms that first night had been more than mind-blowing sex.

Maybe it had been love, even then.

What did it matter? She loved her husband. He was everything she'd wanted without ever knowing she'd wanted it.

There'd been a man, once, when she was in college. He'd talked of a future together. Of how he'd be there for her, supportive of her pursuing a career despite being married.

It had all sounded wonderful until it was time to apply to grad school and she told him about her grandfather, about how he thought her attending graduate school was foolish. About how hard she was going to have to work to change his mind about letting a woman inherit SCB.

You mean, you might not inherit the company? he'd said.

That night, he'd dropped her at the apartment she shared with three other women.

I'll call you, he'd told her.

He never did.

He'd been her one lover, until the night she met Nicolo.

Nicolo, who wanted her. Not what she could bring him. Nicolo, who she loved with all her heart.

She wanted to tell him. Wanted to take his face between her hands, look into his eyes and say, *Nico, my husband, I adore you....*

But she couldn't. She was a liberated woman with two degrees, a woman who could hold her own in the toughest business crowd but when it came to love, she couldn't say the words without hearing them first.

Someday soon, Nicolo would say them.

He would tell her he loved her because, surely, he did. His actions, his lovemaking, his sacrifice of her grandfather's bank...

Why would a man do those things, if not for love?

It was only a matter of time before he said the words.

Except—except, as time slipped past, doubt crept in. Nicolo was the same. Kind, tender, generous. Passionate.

So passionate, even as her belly grew more rounded, that there were times she wept with joy as she came in his arms.

But a little voice had started whispering things she didn't want to hear.

Are you sure, Aimee? it would say slyly. *Will he really tell you he loves you? Are you sure he's not just manipulating you the way your grandfather did all those years he let you think you'd take over at the bank?*

James's lie kept you docile.

Maybe this is Nicolo's lie. To tame you. To keep you warming his bed.

The thoughts were ugly. And untrue. Absolutely untrue. Aimee blocked them out…but sometimes, in the darkest part of the night, the voice still whispered to her and when it did, her heart turned cold.

Her birthday was fast approaching.

Nicolo reminded her of it.

"How did you know?" she said, and he gave her a smug grin and said he'd known it from the day they married. "It's on your passport, remember? Tucked away in my safe."

It was, he said, an important birthday.

"Twenty-five," she said, and gave a dramatic sigh. "A quarter of a century."

Nicolo laughed and caught her up in his arms. "I'm serious, *cara*. It is important." His eyes darkened. "I want you to have a very special day. We'll drive north, to Tuscany. I have a house there. It's much smaller than the *palazzo*, very quiet, very private…" He smiled. "I'll take you to my favorite little *trattoria* so you can practice your Italian by ordering all the local dishes."

She smiled back at him. "It sounds wonderful. I can't wait."

"And I can't wait to see your face when I give you your

birthday present. I think—I know—it will make you very happy."

He put her on her feet. Aimee lay her hand over her belly.

"You've already given me the best gift in the world," she said softly.

Nicolo put his hand over hers just as the baby gave its first kick. She knew she'd never forget the incredulous look that came over his face.

"Was that my son?"

"Or your daughter."

He kissed her. And after that, she stopped listening to that sly little voice because, without question, what it said was a lie.

CHAPTER THIRTEEN

AIMEE'S BIRTHDAY fell on a Saturday.

Which was, Nicolo said, perfect for their visit at the house in Tuscany.

"There's an infinity pool and a hot tub, and a terrace that looks out over the valley. No servants, just a housekeeper who comes in only a couple of times a week." He took Aimee in his arms and kissed her. "We'll have all the privacy we could want, *cara,* so I can teach you some new words in my language and, better yet, show you exactly what they mean. How does that sound?"

It sounded wonderful. Almost too wonderful to be true, but then, the last several weeks had all been like that.

The only thing that could be more perfect would be if Nicolo said he loved her. Aimee hoped that might be the special gift he had for her. A sweet declaration of his love.

Then, life would be perfect.

They planned to leave early Friday morning but Nicolo had to go to his office first to sort out a minor emergency.

Aimee walked him out the front door.

"I'll be back in an hour, no more," he said, as he kissed her goodbye.

"Not a minute more," she answered, kissing him back.

He smiled, but then his expression grew serious. "Are you happy here, with me, *cara?*"

She answered by pressing her mouth to his again.

"Sometimes," he said, his arms tightening around her, "sometimes I think it was fate that sent you on a collision course with me in front of that hotel, and sent us to the same club that evening." He took her face in his hands. "And, lately, I think, too, that we should repay fate's kindness to us by making peace with your grandfather."

Aimee sighed. "I know. I've thought about it. He's old. And frail. And I suppose, in his own way, he did what he thought was right."

Nicolo brushed his mouth gently over hers.

"I am glad you feel that way, *cara,* because—because that plays into my birthday gift for you."

"Making peace with James? I don't understand."

"You will," he said, and kissed her again. "I will explain this weekend, I promise."

"Nicolo! That's not fair. At least give me a hint."

"A hint. Hmm." He grinned. "All right." He put his hand on her rounded belly. "Part of your gift is as much a gift for our baby as for you."

"Some hint! I'm more confused than before!"

Nicolo rolled his eyes. "One more hint, woman, and then my lips are sealed. Let's see…" He took her hand, turned it over and touched his finger to a line across her palm. "I see a journey in your future," he said, his tone as solemn as any fortune-teller's. Then he looked up and grinned. "No more questions, *Principessa.* Nicolo the *Magnifico* has finished telling the future for now."

Aimee laughed. "You're a hard man, Nicolo the Magnificent."

"And you are soft, *cara,*" he said huskily, "as soft as silk in my arms."

A long, deep kiss. Then he trotted down the steps, got into his Ferrari and roared away.

She looked after the car until it vanished through the gates. Then she went back into the *palazzo*, out onto the terrace overlooking the rear gardens, smiling as she gazed over the riotous colors of the flowers.

A hint? Nicolo had given it all away. Her "special birthday gift" was a trip to New York and a reconciliation with James.

It was a generous gesture for her husband to make.

Nicolo was a proud man. Her grandfather's attempt to manipulate him had backfired because of that pride. Now, he'd overlook it and make peace for her sake, and for the sake of their child.

"You're a good man, Nico," she whispered softly. "A wonderful man—"

"Signora?"

Aimee turned around. "Yes, Anna?"

"I have finished packing your suitcase."

"Thank you." Ridiculous, really. She was perfectly capable of packing her own things but Nicolo insisted Anna do it. The further she went in her pregnancy, the more convinced he was that she needed to be treated with extra care.

"I put in all the things you asked for. The cotton tops, the linen trousers. But I wonder... Will you and the *Principe* be dining out? Shall I pack some long gowns? An evening purse? Shoes?"

It was an excellent question and only Nicolo knew the answer.

"I don't know," Aimee said with a little laugh. "Thank you for thinking of it. I'll phone my husband and ask."

The nearest telephone was in Nicolo's study. She'd been in the room often, sitting curled in a corner of the sofa, reading, while he did e-mail. Now, for the first time, she went behind her husband's oversize antique desk, sat in his chair, reached for the phone and dialed his office.

Nicolo picked up after a few rings.

"*Cara?* Are you all right?"

"I'm perfectly fine."

"Good. Good. For a moment, I thought—"

"Nico," she said gently, "really, I'm okay. I just wanted to ask if—"

"I'm on the phone with Paris. May I put you on hold for a few minutes?"

She assured him that he could and settled back to wait.

Soft music played over the telephone line and Aimee hummed along, dah-dah-dahing just a little off-key. Still humming, she plucked a pencil from the desk, pulled a scrap of paper toward her, began to draw stick-figure babies and mommies and daddies….

And stopped.

What was that?

A fax. A fax on her grandfather's letterhead, dated two days after she had married Nicolo.

My dear Prince Barbieri. Once again, let me repeat what I told you when you telephoned. I am delighted by the news of your marriage to my granddaughter…

Well, she knew what this would be about. It was James's response to Nicolo telling him he would not be purchasing the bank.

I am equally delighted by your reminder of my commitment to sell you Stafford-Coleridge-Black.

The pencil dropped to the desk from Aimee's suddenly nerveless fingers.

*I also wish to assure you that I am moving forward
with the paperwork necessary to proceed with the
sale. It will take a few weeks but I assure you,
Principe, everything will go forward as promised.*

Aimee's heart gave a wild lurch.

Nicolo had never told her grandfather he would not
buy SCB? No. It had to be a mistake….

It wasn't.

The proof was just under the fax, contained in a legal
document pages and pages long.

The last page was the one that mattered. It stated that
Barbieri International was now the owner of Stafford-
Coleridge-Black.

Aimee's hand flew to her mouth.

God. Oh dear God! Her husband had lied to her. Lied,
even as he'd held her in his arms and vowed there would
never be any lies between them.

The bank was his. That was why he'd married her after
all. For the bank. And telling her about it was to be her
special birthday present.

He couldn't keep it a secret forever. Mention of the sale
was bound to turn up in magazines and newspapers.
Nicolo had to break the news to her before that happened.

That was the reason he was taking her away.

Her husband would spend the weekend making love to
her. And when she was completely dazzled by all the hours
in his arms, he'd tell her what he'd done. That he'd bought
the bank. He'd make it sound as if he'd just done it, and
that he'd done it solely to reconcile her with her grandfather.

He'd say that he'd done it for her. And that would be
the biggest lie of all.

Everything, *everything* he'd done, was for himself. It had

all been in preparation for this moment. His supposed concern for her. His affection for her. His love for her and, all right, he'd never used the word but she'd begun believing that he loved her, that he wanted her for herself, not for the bank....

"Cara?"

The bank. The horrible bank. The bank that had always been more important than she was, first to James, now to Nicolo—

"Cara? Are you there?"

Aimee's throat was tight. Not with sorrow. With anger. With rage. Bone deep, hot-blooded rage.

"I'm here, Prince Barbieri," she said in a low voice. "But not for long."

"What? Aimee? Aimee—"

She dropped the phone. Ran up the stairs to the bedroom. To her husband's bedroom, a room she'd willingly shared because she'd believed in him, in the life she'd thought they were building together.

Her suitcase was on the bed.

She upended it, threw open her dressing room doors, yanked clothes from their hangers, clothes she'd brought with her from New York; tossed them into the suitcase and, damn it, she was blinking back tears. Tears, and for what? She was angry, not hurting.

Oh God, not hurting!

A sob broke from her throat. Quickly she forced the suitcase shut, grabbed it and ran from the room.

She was halfway down the stairs when Anna looked up and saw her.

"Principessa!" Anna's voice was filled with horror. *"Principessa.* What are you doing? You cannot carry that by yourself."

"I *am* carrying it," Aimee said. "Just watch me."

"But *Principessa*... Giorgio? Giorgio, *venuto qui!* Quickly, Giorgio!"

Giorgio, looking bewildered, hurried toward Anna from the kitchen wing.

"Giorgio." Aimee took a breath. "Good. I wish to go to the airport."

The man stared at her.

"The airport, Giorgio. I want you to take me there."

He looked at her blankly.

"*L'aeroporto, capite?* Damn it, I know you understand!"

"*Principessa.*" Anna was wringing her hands in distress. "*Per favore,* I cannot let you do this. The *principe—*"

"To hell with the *principe!* Tell Giorgio to take me to the airport or I'll go out the door and start walking."

Anna swallowed audibly. So did Giorgio. Aimee ran down the rest of the stairs and brushed past them.

"*Attesta!*" Giorgio shouted. "I will do it."

A moment later, they were speeding out the gates in the big Mercedes, the *palazzo* a blur on the horizon.

Aimee chose an airline at random.

Giorgio wanted to park the Mercedes so he could carry her suitcase inside but she told him to pull to the curb. Once he did, she got out of the car and ran into the terminal.

Soon, she knew, she'd be out of time.

Nicolo would come after her. It would put a dent in his pride if he let her run away.

Fate was cooperating. There was no one in line at the ticket counter. Yes, there was a flight to New York this morning. Yes, there was an available seat.

Thank goodness, Aimee still had her old credit card... But she didn't have her passport.

"I am sorry, Ms. Black," the clerk said politely, "but I cannot issue a ticket if you have no passport."

"I have one," Aimee said desperately, "but I can't get at it. My husband—"

The clerk's polite mask gave way to a look of empathy.

"I understand, but there's nothing I can do. Are you American? Perhaps if you go to your embassy—"

"They won't help me. My husband is—my husband is—"

"I am her husband," an imperious voice growled.

Aimee spun around. Nicolo stood just behind her, his eyes black with tightly controlled anger.

"I am Principe Nicolo Antonius Barbieri," he said. "And my wife is correct. Her embassy cannot help her." His hand closed, hard, on Aimee's elbow. "No one can help her," he said coldly, "because she belongs to me."

"Let go," Aimee panted. "Let go, Nicolo, or—"

"Or what?" His lips drew back from his teeth. "Do you think making a scene will help you? I promise, it will not. Do you remember how Giorgio clicks his heels and salutes me?" His mouth twisted. "The police will do the same. This is my country, and I am a prince."

Aimee stared at the cold, arrogant stranger who was her husband.

"I hate you," she said in a low voice. "I despise you, Nicolo! Do you know that?"

He grabbed her suitcase, tightened his hold on her elbow and started walking. She had no choice but to follow.

He led her out of the terminal. His Ferrari was at the curb, the big Mercedes just ahead of it.

Giorgio sprang from the car, opened the rear door, took one look at his employer's face and scrambled into his seat behind the wheel.

"Get in."

"I will not get in! I'm leaving. There's nothing you can do to stop—"

Nicolo snarled a word, picked her up and put her in the car. Then he climbed in beside her and banged a fist on the closed privacy partition. The Mercedes leaped away and merged into the traffic exiting the airport.

"Now," he said, turning his hot, furious gaze on Aimee, "tell me what you think you are doing."

"Tell Giorgio to turn this car around." Aimee shot to the edge of her seat and pounded on the partition. "Giorgio? Take me back to the airport."

There was no response. The car kept moving forward.

"I'm leaving you, Nicolo," Aimee said. "Do you hear me? I am leaving you, and there's nothing you can do to stop me."

"I won't have to do a thing." Nicolo folded his arms. "Customs will do it for me. You have no passport."

"I'll get one. I'll phone the American Embassy. They won't give a damn that you call yourself a prince, especially when I tell them that you're really an arrogant, deceitful, lying—"

"Be careful, *cara*. It is not wise to add fuel to a fire that is already burning."

It was hard, being so close to him. Looking into the eyes she'd foolishly let herself believe shone with love for her.

His eyes were cold now. Cold and flat and empty.

Suddenly Aimee felt almost unbearably weary. He was right. He was a prince. A macho male. He held all the cards; she held none. He'd lied to her. Hurt her in the worst possible way but he'd shown her kindness, too.

There had to be a shred of kindness left for her in his heart.

Aimee sank back against the seat.

"Don't do this," she whispered. "Please, Nicolo. Just let me go."

"There was a time you called me Nico."

She looked at him. His voice was low; the anger in his eyes had been replaced by bewilderment... But he was a good actor. She knew that better than anyone.

"A mistake," she said. "Everything was a mistake."

"*Cara.* I do not understand. I left, you were happy. The next thing I know—"

"The next thing you know," she said, trying to sound cold, trying not to give way to tears, "the next thing you know, the game's up."

"What game? What are you talking about?"

"Your game. This game. You and me." She took a deep breath. "It's over. I don't want you anymore."

"Why do you not want me? What happened?"

"I came to my senses, is what happened."

"Meaning?"

"Meaning, I realized what a—a joke this has been. You. Me. This farce of a marriage."

"Is that what our marriage is to you? A joke?"

Another change of tone. There was warning in it now but Aimee was beyond heeding that warning.

"You know it is."

She cried out as he pulled her to him. His lips crushed hers; his kiss was savage and deep but it didn't touch her heart.

He had lost his power to seduce her.

He would never have that power again...except, except, God, she was going to cry.

Going to?

She was crying already, tears burning her eyes as she fought against them and she didn't want to give him the satisfaction of seeing her weep because—because there was nothing to weep about. She didn't love him, she'd never loved him—

"I don't love you," she gasped, tearing her mouth from his.

The words came out before she could stop them. Nicolo raised his eyebrows.

"Strange. How could you not love me when you never claimed to love me?"

"I meant—I meant I didn't love you, even when I thought I did."

"Yet you never said those words to me."

"I said, I *thought* I loved you. But I didn't. It was all sex. You knew that. You used it against me."

"I see. I used sex to make you fall in love with me."

"Yes. No. I didn't fall in love with you. Damn it, you're twisting everything, the way you always do."

"What have I twisted in the past?"

"You know damned well what you twisted. And I'm not going to do this! I'm not going to give you the chance to try to convince me not to leave you because I've made up my mind. I *am* leaving you—and you won't lose a thing, because the bank is already in your pocket!"

Nicolo cocked his head. "Really? The bank is in my pocket?"

Aimee slammed her fist against his chest. "Don't," she cried. "Don't make fun of me. Don't lie! Don't, don't, don't…"

Tears began streaming down her face.

You could only pretend to hate the man who owned your heart for just so long and then the enormity of losing him, of having been a pawn that meant nothing to him, became too painful to bear.

She sagged against his hands.

"Please," she said brokenly, "please, Nicolo, if you have any feeling at all for me, let me go."

"*Cara.*" His arms went around her; he gathered her close despite her struggles and drew her into his lap. "Tell me what happened. What hurt you. Tell me, so I can make it go away."

"What happened," she said as a shudder racked her body, "is that I discovered the truth."

"No," he said gently, "I don't think that's possible because if you knew the truth, if I had told it to you a long time ago, you would not be weeping in my arms."

"I'm not weeping," Aimee said, her body shaking with her sobs.

"Of course not. You're too strong to cry. Isn't that right, *cara?*" His smile tilted as he took a white linen square from his pocket and handed it to her. "I told you I'd work up to a handkerchief someday."

Aimee wiped her eyes, blew her nose, then balled the hankie in her fist. "Now. What is this truth that has made you want to leave me?"

She lifted her head and met his eyes. "I found the fax."

"What fax?"

"The one from my grandfather, assuring you he'd sell the bank to you."

His face fell. "Ah."

"Yes. Ah, indeed. I found everything. That fax—and the papers that showed the sale had gone through."

"What else did you find?"

His tone was neutral. At least he wasn't going to try to deny the truth.

"Isn't that enough?" Her voice broke. "I'd married you. I'd agreed to live with you, to be your wife. Why did you have to lie? Why did you tell me you weren't going to buy the bank? Why did you make me fall—make me fall—"

"What, *cara?*" Tenderly he brushed her honeyed curls back from her cheeks. "What did I make you do?"

Why hide it now? Her pride lay in tatters; by the end of this, she would have none left to lose. Then she would leave him. She couldn't live this way, loving him and knowing he had never loved her.

And yes, she loved him. Despite everything, she loved him. She would always love him.

"Cara," Nicolo said softly, "are you telling me that you love me?"

She didn't answer.

And, for the first time in his life, Nicolo found himself terrified of what a woman's answer might be because if his wife didn't say that she loved him—

If she didn't, he would be lost.

Lost, because he loved her with all his heart. He would always love her. The vows they had taken said it would be until death, but that was wrong.

He would love her until then, and beyond.

Months ago, a woman had run into him on the street and she'd left him in a rage he hadn't been able to understand.

When he saw her again, in a club that same night, his rage had changed to desire so savage it had baffled him.

And, through the twists and turns of destiny, he had married her.

He'd told himself he'd done it for the child they'd created but even then, deep inside, he'd known that he'd done it for a simpler reason.

He loved her.

And that love had grown until it was the most important thing in his life. But he was too much an idiot—all right, too much a coward to admit it.

After all, he had never loved anyone before.

No. That wasn't true. He'd loved his parents, but they had not loved him. He'd loved his *gran-nonna,* but she had died. He'd even loved a couple of his governesses, but they'd disappeared like puffs of smoke.

He would not, could not make himself that vulnerable again.

Instead he'd come up with ways to show what he felt for his wife. The engagement ring. The wedding bands. *Dio,* he had never thought he'd want to wear a ring. Wasn't a ring a more civilized version of shackles?

It turned out it was not. A ring was a way of telling the world he adored his wife.

His problem then had been telling the same thing to his wife. Words had terrified him. Suppose she hadn't felt the same? So he'd come up with what had seemed a clever plan.

He'd tell her grandfather he didn't want to buy the bank.

Good, as far as it went. His Aimee's smile, when he told her what he'd done, had filled him with happiness....

Then, a little while later, he'd thought of something even better. He'd buy the bank, then give it to his wife as a gift.

So clever. So brilliant...

So stupid.

His plan had backfired. And now, his wife wanted to leave him.

No, he thought fiercely, no....

"Aimee." Nicolo took a deep breath. "I asked you a question, *cara.* I asked if you love me."

"Nicolo—"

"But that was wrong. I should have spoken first. I should have said—I should have told you that I adore you, *bellissima mia.* That I cannot imagine living without you." She shook her head, turned it away and he cupped her chin, gently but firmly forced her to look at him. "You are my heart, Aimee. You are my life."

"Nicolo. I *saw* the papers. I saw—"

The Mercedes had stopped a long time ago. Nicolo looked out, saw the broad steps that led into the *palazzo*. Giorgio, clever man, was nowhere in sight but the front door of the *palazzo* stood open.

Nicolo carried his wife from the car, up the steps and into the house. She told him to put her down but he kissed her to silence, carried her into his study and gently set her on her feet, though he wasn't taking any chances.

He kept his arm around her while he rifled through the papers on his desk, found the one he wanted and held it out to her.

"What is that?"

"It is the gift I intended to give you this weekend, the gift I hoped would take the place of the words I was too much a coward to say, that I love you, I need you, that I cannot live without you."

Aimee looked up at him, her eyes still awash in tears.

"Read it," he said gently. "*Per favore,* sweetheart, I beg you. Read it."

Slowly Aimee took the document from him and began to read. Halfway through, she blinked. Looked up and shook her head.

"Nicolo. I don't understand. This says—"

"It says that the damnable bank is yours, *amante.*"

"But it can't be. My grandfather—"

"Sold it to me. And as soon as it was mine, I told my attorneys to change the name of the owner from Barbieri International to Aimee Black Barbieri." His voice softened. "It should always have been yours, *cara.* And now, it is."

"You mean, you bought it just so you—"

"*Si.* It is my gift to you, a gift I give you with all the love in my heart, now and forever. You must believe me. I love you, love you, love you—"

And then Aimee was in his arms, her mouth on his, and the papers transferring SCB from husband to wife were on the floor where they belonged, because nothing was or would ever be as important as the love between Prince Nicolo Antonius Barbieri and his princess....

At least, nothing as important until the birth of a little prince a few months later.

His name was Nicolo James Antonius Barbieri and, yes, he was named for his father and his grandfather because it was amazing how news of his only granddaughter's pregnancy had mellowed a stern, cold old man.

And when little Nicolo—Nickie, to his adoring parents—was two weeks old, he attended the first big event of his life.

The marriage, the real marriage of his mother and father because, his papa said, a beautiful woman deserved a beautiful wedding.

Aimee carried a bouquet of white roses and pink orchids, from the *palazzo's* greenhouse. Her gown was made of cream antique lace and had a flowing train.

Nicolo wore a black dinner suit with a white rosebud in his lapel.

The baby wore white, too, a little silk suit handmade by Anna, who wept when she was asked to be the baby's godmother.

The ceremony was held in the conservatory of the *palazzo*, lit by hundreds of white candles, scented by thousands of white roses while a string quartet played softly in the background.

It was a small wedding, attended only by James Black, a couple of Aimee's friends from her college days and, of course, the groom's two confirmed bachelor pals, a Spaniard named Lucas and a Greek named Damian. They slapped Nicolo's back, kissed his bride, said how happy they were for them both and agreed, in low voices over glasses of excellent *vino,* that marriage was okay for Nicolo but it would never be right for them.

Although, Damian admitted, Nicolo certainly did seem happy.

Just look at how he was smiling. At how he kissed his son good-night when Anna said it was time for her to put the baby to bed. At how he danced with his wife, and how he swept her into his arms midway through the evening, kissed her, then carried her through the conservatory and into the *palazzo.*

"Time for a toast," Lucas said, raising his glass.

Damian looked at him and grinned. They both knew exactly how the old toast was supposed to go, but not tonight.

Not ever again, where Nicolo was concerned.

"To Nicolo," Lucas said.

The men touched glasses.

"And to Aimee," Damian added. "May they live happily ever after."

The guests cheered, and the sound carried through the softness of the night and through the open windows of the second-floor bedroom where Nicolo was just putting his bride on her feet.

"I love you," he whispered against her mouth.

"Ti amo," she said, against his.

Then he drew her down into their bed where they made that vow of love again, this time with their bodies, their souls and their hearts.

The big miniseries from

Bedded by *Blackmail*

Forced to bed...then to wed?

Dare you read it?

He's got her firmly in his sights
and she has only one chance
of survival—surrender to his
blackmail...and him...in his bed!

September's arrival:

BLACKMAILED INTO
THE ITALIAN'S BED
by Miranda Lee

Jordan had struggled to forget Gino Bortelli,
but suddenly the arrogant, sexy Italian was back,
and he was determined to have Jordan in his bed again....

Coming in October:

WILLINGLY BEDDED,
FORCIBLY WEDDED
by Melanie Milburne
Book #2673

HARLEQUIN®

Mediterranean
N I G H T S™

Experience glamour, elegance, mystery and revenge
aboard the high seas....

Coming in September 2007...

BREAKING ALL
THE RULES

by

Marisa Carroll

Aboard the cruise ship *Alexandra's Dream* for
some R & R, sports journalist Lola Sandler is
surprised to spot pro-golfer Eric Lashman.
Years after walking away from the pro circuit
with no explanation to the public, Eric now
finds himself teaching aboard a cruise ship.

Lola smells a career-making exposé...
but their developing relationship may
force her to make a difficult choice.

www.eHarlequin.com   HM38963

REQUEST YOUR FREE BOOKS!

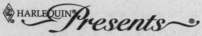

2 FREE NOVELS PLUS 2
FREE GIFTS!

YES! Please send me 2 FREE Harlequin Presents® novels and my 2 FREE gifts. After receiving them, if I don't wish to receive any more books, I can return the shipping statement marked "cancel." If I don't cancel, I will receive 6 brand-new novels every month and be billed just $3.80 per book in the U.S., or $4.47 per book in Canada, plus 25¢ shipping and handling per book and applicable taxes, if any*. That's a savings of close to 15% off the cover price! I understand that accepting the 2 free books and gifts places me under no obligation to buy anything. I can always return a shipment and cancel at any time. Even if I never buy another book from Harlequin, the two free books and gifts are mine to keep forever.

106 HDN EEXK 306 HDN EEXV

Name	(PLEASE PRINT)	
Address		Apt. #
City	State/Prov.	Zip/Postal Code

Signature (if under 18, a parent or guardian must sign)

Mail to the **Harlequin Reader Service®**:
IN U.S.A.: P.O. Box 1867, Buffalo, NY 14240-1867
IN CANADA: P.O. Box 609, Fort Erie, Ontario L2A 5X3

Not valid to current Harlequin Presents subscribers.

Want to try two free books from another line?
Call 1-800-873-8635 or visit www.morefreebooks.com.

* Terms and prices subject to change without notice. NY residents add applicable sales tax. Canadian residents will be charged applicable provincial taxes and GST. This offer is limited to one order per household. All orders subject to approval. Credit or debit balances in a customer's account(s) may be offset by any other outstanding balance owed by or to the customer. Please allow 4 to 6 weeks for delivery.

Your Privacy: Harlequin is committed to protecting your privacy. Our Privacy Policy is available online at www.eHarlequin.com or upon request from the Reader Service. From time to time we make our lists of customers available to reputable firms who may have a product or service of interest to you. If you would prefer we not share your name and address, please check here. ☐

HP07

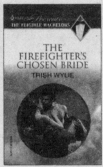

Always passionate, always proud.

· **The richest royal family in the world—
a family united by blood and passion,
torn apart by deceit and desire.**

By royal decree, Harlequin Presents is delighted to bring
you The Royal House of Niroli. Step into the glamorous,
enticing world of the Nirolian Royal Family. As the king
ails he must find an heir. Each month an exciting new
installment follows the epic search for the true Nirolian
king. Eight heirs, eight romances, eight fantastic stories!

Coming in September:

BOUGHT BY THE BILLIONAIRE PRINCE
by Carol Marinelli

Luca Fierezza is ruthless, a rogue and a rebel....
Megan Donavan's stunned when she's thrown into
jail and her unlikely rescuer is her new boss, Luca!
But now she's also entirely at his mercy...in his bed!

**Be sure not to miss any of the passion!
Coming in October:**

THE TYCOON'S PRINCESS BRIDE
by Natasha Oakley

www.eHarlequin.com

HP12659